A SCOTTISH FLING

AN ELIZA THOMSON INVESTIGATES MURDER MYSTERY

VL MCBEATH

A Scottish Fling
By VL McBeath

For more about this author please visit:
https://vlmcbeath.com

https://vlmcbeath.com/contact/

*

Editing services provided by Susan Cunningham (www.perfectproseservices.com)
Cover design by Michelle Abrahall (www.michelleabrahall.com)

ISBNs:
978-1-9161340-4-1 (Kindle Edition)
978-1-9161340-5-8 (Paperback)

Main category - FICTION / Historical Mysteries
Other category - FICTION / Crime & Mystery

Previous books in the *Eliza Thomson Investigates* series

Introductory Novella: *A Deadly Tonic*
Murder in Moreton
Death of an Honourable Gent
Dying for a Garden Party
A Christmas Murder (A Novella)

Get your FREE copy of *A Deadly Tonic.*

Sign up to the *Eliza Thomson Investigates* newsletter for further information and exclusive content about the series.

Details can be found at **www.vlmcbeath.com**

DR ARCHIE THOMSON'S FAMILY

Eliza Thomson: Wife
Henry Thomson: Son

Mr & Mrs Thomson: Father & mother (pa & ma)

Fraser Thomson: Brother
Rabbie and Callum: Fraser's sons

Jean Stewart: Sister
Mr Stewart: Jean's Husband
Niall and Ross: Jean's sons

Maggie Scott: Sister
Mr Robert Scott: Maggie's husband
Flora and Caitlin: Maggie's daughters
Mrs Scott: Maggie's mother-in-law

CHAPTER ONE

August 1902

I t had taken eight hours, but finally the train pulled into St Andrews, the railway station they'd been longing to see. Eliza stood up as a porter entered their compartment to collect the luggage.

"Whoever said the railways have made life easier have never made the journey from London to the outer regions of Scotland." Her humour had deserted her within an hour of leaving Edinburgh, and she grimaced as husband Archie offered her a hand to climb down from the train. "Father's got a lot to answer for."

"In fairness, he hasn't been further than Edinburgh." Archie released her hand and waited for her friend Connie Appleton to appear by the door.

"Getting to Edinburgh was bad enough, but it was a breeze compared to this latest journey. Why we had to wait so long to change trains in the middle of nowhere, I'll never know. Has nobody thought to hold one train back until the other one arrives?"

"At least we're here now." Connie joined Eliza on the platform before her eyes darted to Archie. "We are in the right place, aren't we?"

"Nearly."

"Nearly?" Eliza put the back of a hand to her forehead. "How much further?"

"Only about twenty minutes. Your transport awaits." He pointed to two horses standing in front of a covered carriage. "We're in St Andrews and just need to go around the headland to our little village of St Giles."

Eliza gazed straight ahead. "Why couldn't you have been born in Edinburgh? It would have made life so much easier."

"If I'd been from Edinburgh I may never have travelled to London to study medicine, so thank your lucky stars I'm not." Archie grinned at Eliza's attempt at a scowl. "Why don't you and Connie settle yourselves into the carriage while Henry and I bring over the bags."

Eliza eyed her son as he jumped from the train and studied the luggage blocking the exit from the station.

"Can't we find a porter?" He scratched his head as he turned to face them.

"Around here?" Eliza gestured to the row of trees on the grass bank opposite the platform. "I doubt it."

"You wait and see." Henry gazed in the opposite direction. "There must be a coachman, at least; I'll see if he'll help."

Before Eliza could answer, Henry was heading towards the road, leaving his parents to watch after him.

"You need to have a word with him. Your mother won't take kindly to him wanting everything done for him."

Archie laughed. "Nonsense, she'll love it. She hasn't seen him since he was a boy and now he's studying medicine..."

"I know, he'll be just like his father, unable to do any wrong." Eliza linked her arm through Connie's. "Thank goodness I persuaded you to come with us. It's the only way I'll be able to escape."

Connie's pale blue eyes narrowed. "Where are we going?"

"Anywhere. You know Archie's mother doesn't care for me, so you're my excuse to avoid having to sit with her for hours. You like to walk, so we'll explore the village."

Archie laughed. "That won't take long."

"Well, we'll do it more than once."

Connie frowned as Eliza directed her towards the carriage. "We're not staying with them, are we?"

"We are not, but it's a small village."

Archie was still within earshot. "You're not staying away from her for the whole ten days."

"I know, but I don't have to visit as often as you do." Eliza stopped when she reached the horses. "Only twenty more minutes of freedom."

It was a further ten minutes before the coachman loaded the last of the luggage and Archie and Henry joined them.

"That took a long time."

Archie settled into the seat facing his wife. "People don't rush up here. Just relax and take in the air. As soon as we leave the station, the sea will come into view and you'll see the scenery. My biggest worry is that you'll like it so much that you won't want to go home."

Eliza snorted. "I doubt that very much. Give me my

village close to London any time. Besides, we can't let Connie travel home on her own."

Connie's eyes widened. "You wouldn't really stay, would you?"

"Of course we wouldn't. We can't have Sergeant Cooper wondering where you've disappeared to."

"Eliza!" Connie's cheeks flushed. "He's just a friend. Besides, he knows where we are."

"Just a friend?" Archie frowned. "I thought it was more than that."

"What have I missed?" Henry said. "Are you and Sergeant Cooper walking out together?"

Connie rolled her shoulders and folded her hands in her lap. "No, we're not, we're just friends. Nothing more than that."

"Ah." Archie winked at Eliza.

"Leave her alone ... and not a word to Sergeant Cooper. He'd be terribly upset if he knew they were only friends."

"Is that the sea over there?" Connie pointed to the unmistakable mass of water, ignoring the smirks on Archie and Henry's faces.

"It most certainly is." Archie followed her gaze. "My, it's good to be back. As nice as Moreton is, the pond at the end of the village can't compete. The golf course here is one of the best, too."

Connie swivelled back to face Archie. "I didn't know you played golf, Dr Thomson."

"I haven't for many a year, but I'm sure I can find someone to give me a game. I could even teach Henry to play. It'll give the two of you time to sit with Mother."

"Don't get any ideas." There was no hint of humour in Eliza's voice.

"Doesn't it take hours to play a game of golf?" Connie's brow furrowed.

"Yes, it does, and he's kidding ... aren't you?" Eliza glared at her husband. "You can't go leaving us for hours on end. Your mother won't want to spend time with me any more than I do with her."

"Don't be so silly. She'll have forgiven you for keeping me in London; I told her it was your idea to visit, so I imagine you'll be in her good books."

"When did you tell her that?"

"When I wrote to say we were visiting."

"Did you also mention it was my idea to stay at the local inn?"

Archie grimaced. "No, I took the blame for that. I told them they wouldn't have enough room for four of us. Despite what you think, I do consider these things, so will you please cheer up."

Eliza settled back in her seat and watched the coast pass by until they came into some houses. Several minutes later they pulled up outside The Coach House, an inn in the centre of the village.

Eliza tightened her shawl around her shoulders as the coachman opened the door.

"Another drawback of Scotland is it's always so much colder than London."

Archie let out a deep sigh. "Are you going to moan for the next ten days? You were the one who suggested we come and now we're here, we're going to be sociable and enjoy ourselves. Is that too much to ask?"

"I'm sorry. I'm just tired after almost nine hours on the train to Edinburgh and then another eight hours to get here. You can't blame me. If we could just get a cup of tea, I'm sure it would help."

"Well, make sure it does. We need to visit Ma and Pa once we settle in."

Eliza wasn't used to Archie chastising her and her cheeks burned as she climbed down from the carriage and headed into the inn.

"Wait for me." Connie chased after her. "I'll order the tea while you sit down."

"You'll do no such thing." Archie ushered the two of them across the room to a table beside the fire. "I'll sort everything out."

Eliza chose the seat against the wall and cast her eyes around the room, noting the dents in its wood-panelled walls and the array of stools surrounding the bar in the opposite corner. "That window could do with being bigger." She nodded to the front of the room. "It's too dark in here for my liking, but I don't suppose we'll be able to stay once it opens to the villagers."

"I should hope we won't." Connie swivelled around on her wooden chair to take in the surroundings. "We shouldn't be in here at the same time as the locals, and besides, these chairs aren't very comfortable."

"It's to be hoped the bedrooms are pleasant enough then. I get the impression we'll be spending a lot of time in them."

"Oh, I do hope not." Connie pouted as she sank back into her seat. "I know we'll be visiting relatives, but can't we go walking along the beach, too?"

"We most certainly can." A faint smile crossed Eliza's lips

as she watched Archie in the hallway beyond the door. He stood at a table that served as a reception desk. Even with his greying hair, he was still a handsome man. Henry, who stood with him, had more than a look of him. She had to cheer up. It wasn't like her to be so down. She nodded towards her husband. "He's been looking forward to coming for weeks. He hasn't seen his parents for the last five years."

"It must be hard on his mother," Connie said.

Eliza sighed. "I suppose so. It's bad enough when Henry's away at Cambridge for months at a time. I can't imagine not seeing him for years."

"Well then, let's both put a smile on our faces and make sure he has a nice break."

An unbidden smile flicked across Eliza's lips. "Oh, Connie, you're so sweet. I wish I had your good nature, but at the moment I'm more bothered about being unwelcome. I tell you, if anything's said after the journey we've just had, I won't be happy."

"I'm sure nobody would do such a thing."

"I hope you're right, but when we were here five years ago, his mother left me in no doubt that she'd have been happier if I hadn't bothered travelling. The way I feel at the moment, I'm beginning to wish I'd listened to her and not come. I'm just grateful Archie agreed to you joining us. At least he and Henry can spend time with her without involving me."

"There, that's everything sorted." Archie took the seat next to Eliza while Henry sat beside Connie, his back to the bar. "A double room for us and singles for Henry and Mrs Appleton. We're allowed to use the bar area to eat, but there's a separate dining room on the other side of the hall if we prefer."

"Oh, that's good." Connie pulled her shawl more tightly around her. "I'm not comfortable in a bar."

"Would you like to move?" Archie asked.

"Oh no, not at all. It's pleasant while the inn's closed, but once it's open..."

"I think you'll be fine. It's only half past four and it won't open for another half an hour. Even when it is, it probably doesn't get busy." He squeezed Eliza's hand. "Come on, no more sulking; there's a pot of tea on its way."

Eliza gave him a brief smile. "I'm sorry. I'm just nervous about meeting everyone again."

Archie leaned back as a maid placed a tray containing four cups and saucers, a large pot of tea and a plate of cakes on the table before him. "I don't see you nervous very often. You must either be tired or sickening for something. It's a good job we stayed in Edinburgh for a couple of days before coming up here. Goodness knows what you'd have been like if we'd carried straight on the next morning."

Eliza helped herself to a slice of Dundee Cake. "I'll be fine. Now, let's get this tea poured and we can go and meet everyone. I'm sure I'll settle once we've made the introductions."

CHAPTER TWO

The smile returned to Eliza's face as she finished the cake and washed it down with her second cup of tea. If it was any indication of how good the rest of the food would be, she'd have no complaints.

Archie stood up to help Eliza from her chair. "You can show Mrs Appleton around the village tomorrow, but I think we need to get next door and visit Ma and Pa first."

Henry held open the door as they filed out onto the uneven road and Archie linked Eliza's arm through his.

"I'm afraid there are no footpaths, Mrs Appleton. There's so little traffic around these parts they really aren't necessary. You've no need to worry about walking in the road, though. You won't be going far." He led them down the hill to the first house in a row of cottages. "Here we are, nice and convenient."

Archie knocked on the front door before he stepped into the hallway and popped his head through a door on the right. "Can we come in?"

"Archibald!" Mrs Thomson jumped to her feet and

hurried towards him. "Come here and let your old ma have a look at you."

Archie looked uncomfortable as she threw her arms around him. "That's enough. Don't forget I've brought the family with me." He stepped back and ushered them into the living room. "You remember Eliza?"

Mrs Thomson's face twisted as she looked Eliza up and down. "I'm hardly likely to forget."

"This is Mrs Appleton, Eliza's companion, and..." he turned around to thrust Henry into the centre of the room "... this is Henry. He's a little bigger than when he last visited."

"Oh, my boy, come and stand by the window and let me look at you. My eyes aren't as good as they were, and it never gets light in here. Haven't you grown? Archie, come and stand with him and let me see the two of you together."

"Archie! You're here." A woman a few years older than Eliza, with ginger hair and a freckled complexion, hurried into the room. "It's wonderful to see you again."

Archie held out his hands as she approached. "And you. It's been too long. You remember Eliza?"

"Yes, of course." A smile flickered across the woman's lips.

"Eliza, Mrs Appleton, this is my sister Maggie."

"Yes, I remember. It's lovely to see you again." Eliza gestured towards Connie. "This is my companion, Mrs Appleton; she's never been to Scotland and so we thought it would be a treat for her."

"Well, I'm very glad you could join us."

"Is your husband with you?" Eliza glanced around the room.

"He'll be here shortly. He's not been in long and so he's finishing his dinner."

"Maggie, come here." Mrs Thomson held her grandson's hand as she beckoned Maggie towards them. "This is Henry. Do you remember the last time we saw him? He was nothing but a wee boy, and now he's going to be a doctor. What a blessing to have two doctors in the family."

"Yes, we're very fortunate to live so close to one of the best universities in the country." Eliza found her sweetest smile for her mother-in-law.

"You don't have St Andrews on your doorstep. That's the best there is."

Eliza's smile dropped. *Has she just bitten a lemon?*

Archie held up his hand. "That's enough. Where's Pa?"

"He's out the back; he won't be long. Eliza, Mrs Appleton, please take a seat." Maggie indicated towards two wooden chairs that looked as if they belonged in the kitchen. "Did you know my brother is so revered around here that he's succeeded in bringing Robert's ma back to St Giles?"

"Mrs Scott?" Archie frowned. "She lives miles away, doesn't she?"

"Exactly, and yet thanks to you, she's coming to visit for a week."

Eliza didn't detect any joy in Maggie's words.

"How bizarre; I hardly know her. She must have another reason for making the journey."

Maggie shrugged. "I imagine so, but she hasn't mentioned what it is."

Seeing the confusion on Connie's face, Eliza leaned forward. "Robert is Mr Scott, Maggie's husband."

"Is he not here yet?" An elderly man with stooped shoulders and a gruff voice appeared.

"Pa!" Archie took half a dozen strides across the room

11

before extending his hand. "It's good to be back."

"Aye, and it's as well you're here if it keeps your ma quiet for a few weeks."

Eliza stood up and held out her hand to her father-in-law. "Good evening, Mr Thomson."

Mr Thomson stared at it before grunting and turning back to Archie. "Where's this boy of yours then?"

"Over here." Mrs Thomson had Henry seated in a chair next to hers. "Come and meet him."

"All in good time, woman." He pulled Archie to one side. "Go and sit yourself down; I've a wee spot of Scotch for you."

"You've always got a spot of Scotch." Mrs Thomson rested back in her seat. "Don't pretend to Archibald it's only for special occasions. Shouldn't you wait, though?"

"If Fraser can't be here on time, I'm not waiting for him."

"Fraser's here?" Archie's eyes lit up at the mention of his brother.

"He is." Mrs Thomson's eyes glistened in the firelight. "He usually visits about once a month anyway, but he's made a special journey knowing you'd be here. He stays with Jean and Mr Stewart, but he'll be over any minute. He's got the boys with him, too."

"Gracious, you'll have a full house." Eliza counted the chairs around the room. There was no chance everyone would squeeze on to what was available.

Mrs Thomson flapped her hand. "We've managed before and we'll manage again. Besides, Jean won't come tonight so it will just be me and my boys."

And where are we supposed to go! Eliza rolled her eyes at Connie but turned back around when another voice filled the room.

"Archie!"

"Fraser!" Archie once again bounded across the room. "I wasn't expecting to see you."

"You don't think I'd let you come all this way without paying you a visit, do you? What have you been up to...?"

"Before you two start, I'll get us that drink." Mr Thomson pulled three glasses from a dresser and ushered his sons to the corner of the room near the window. "Maggie, you make a pot of tea for everyone else."

Maggie groaned and turned towards the kitchen, almost bumping into Fraser's sons as she did. "Good grief. Did you two have to come in so quietly?"

"We didn't want to interrupt." It was the taller of the two boys, his fair hair cut neatly around his neck and ears, who spoke. "Not when we don't know everyone."

"There's not many you don't know. This is your Uncle Archie and Aunt Eliza with your cousin Henry. Don't you remember them?"

The boy nodded. "I do now you've mentioned them."

Henry looked relieved when the older boy stepped forward and offered his hand. "I'm Rabbie and this is my brother Callum."

Henry moved away from his grandmother. "I remember now."

Rabbie leaned forward and whispered to Henry before they both smirked and studied the grandfather clock near the door.

"What are you up to, Rabbie Thomson?" Maggie's eyes narrowed as she walked towards the door.

"Nothing. I just asked Henry if he'd like us to show him around while it's still light."

"That's what it's called now, is it?" Maggie winked at Eliza as she headed for the kitchen, causing Eliza to jump up and grab Connie's arm before following her across the hall.

"What was all that about?" Eliza asked as they found Maggie filling the kettle.

She chuckled. "Given their grandfather is unlikely to share any of that Scotch, I imagine they're planning a trip to The Coach House."

Eliza groaned. "They shouldn't encourage him. I had hoped he'd have a quiet two weeks before he goes back to Cambridge."

"I'm sure he'll be fine. They don't drink too much because they take after Pa and won't spend much money."

"That's a relief. Now, may we help you?"

"If you wouldn't mind. I'm not used to serving so many. Archie's attracted everyone this week. He really should come more often."

"So it seems." Eliza studied the well-stocked kitchen with a large wooden table taking centre stage and a range oven and an assortment of cupboards around the edge. She took some cups and saucers from a dresser next to the door.

"Are these the ones you use?"

"Yes, the best china only comes out on a Sunday. Could you stack them on a tray for me?"

"Should I put any out for the boys?"

Maggie chuckled. "I doubt it, they'll be gone before the tea's brewed. I suggested to Pa before you came that he offer them some Scotch now they're all of age, but he wouldn't hear of it. It's hard enough for him to give Archie and Fraser any. Fraser's learned to pace himself; I hope Archie hasn't got too much of a taste for the stuff."

Eliza enjoyed the humour. "No, I'm sure one glass will do him. Besides, with us staying at The Coach House, he can always have a nightcap once we get back."

"If I can get away from Ma, I might join you." Maggie smiled as she shook her head. "She'll be in her element with both of them here. That's why Jean decided not to come tonight, to let Ma have them to herself. I nearly didn't call myself, but I knew she wouldn't want to be making the tea and tidying up herself. Hopefully, I'll speak to Archie as the week goes on."

"I'm sure you will."

"At least Jean always has the excuse that she has the fish to deal with. There must be something going on over there tonight, though, otherwise her boys, Niall and Ross, would be here. They see a lot of Rabbie and Callum and usually go to The Coach House together if they have any spare time."

"You must be busy with Mrs Scott's visit as well. How long is she staying?"

Maggie shuddered. "Don't remind me. A couple of weeks, I hope, although she didn't say in her letter."

"Where's she coming from?" Connie asked.

"Over in Cupar. It takes about an hour to get there in a carriage and so this is a big trip for her."

"Is she travelling alone?"

Maggie took a deep breath. "Don't get me started. Unfortunately, her husband died earlier in the year and now she expects Robert to do everything for her. He has to collect her tomorrow."

"That's a shame."

"More than you know."

"Don't you get on?" Eliza raised an eyebrow.

Maggie shook her head. "That's an understatement. I'll tell you about it later if we get a chance. Anyway, what about you, Mrs Appleton? Have you left Mr Appleton in London or has he travelled with you?"

"No, sadly I'm a widow, too. I have been for over four years now."

"That's a long time. Is there nobody else?"

Connie glanced at Eliza. "No, not yet."

"Well, I don't know what the men in England are up to, an attractive woman like you being on her own for so long."

Eliza chuckled. "Oh, don't worry about her. It's Connie who doesn't want the attention, not the other way around."

"I wanted a respectable period of mourning, you know that."

Maggie picked up the teapot and placed it on the tray. "Well, don't wait too long if you find a nice one. They don't stay single or widowed for long. Not around here at any rate."

Eliza held open the door as Maggie carried the tray through to the living room. Rabbie and Callum stood up as soon as they entered.

"Are you going out already?" Maggie scowled at them. "Henry's not been here half an hour."

Rabbie glanced down at his grandmother, who was fully occupied by Archie and Fraser. "If you don't mention it, she won't miss us."

Callum grinned at his aunt. "We wouldn't go if Grandpa shared his Scotch with us, but I'm sure he'd rather we went out than do that."

Maggie laughed. "Aye, you're right. Off you go."

Eliza gave a subtle nod to Henry as his cousins left. "Go and enjoy yourself. I'm sure we won't be far behind you."

CHAPTER THREE

By one o'clock the following day, Eliza had walked away the tensions of their journey and sampled her first Scottish kippers, and locally grown raspberries with cream. With her dessert plate empty, she dabbed her napkin to her lips and placed it on the table in front of her.

"That was very pleasant, I don't remember when I last had fish for luncheon."

"You'd better get used to it," Archie said. "I imagine you'll be tired of it by the time we leave."

"Well, let me enjoy it for now, at least."

"I don't know that I will." Connie took a sip of water. "The walk along the beach helped build an appetite and so if we do that every day, I'm sure it will help. It really is beautiful around here. It's the sort of view I'd like a painting of to cheer me up on a cold winter morning."

Henry shook his head. "The finished product may be nice, but can you imagine sitting for hours painting it? It must be incredibly dull." He scratched his head. "It's bad enough drawing plants in botany."

Eliza chuckled. "I'm afraid you have my skills when it comes to sketching. I was never very good at it either. Some people find it relaxing, though."

"Hmm. If you say so."

Archie waited for a maid to clear the table. "So, assuming you don't want to find a set of oil paints and spend the afternoon on the headland, I suggest we visit your Aunties Jean and Maggie next. It's easier to talk to them in a small group rather than wait until later when everyone's together."

"Why, what's happening tonight?" Henry stared at his father.

"If you hadn't gone gallivanting last night, you'd know. Your Aunty Jean sent word that we're all invited to sample the latest batch of kippers."

Henry frowned. "More fish. I thought they were usually only for breakfast."

Archie laughed. "In London they are, but up here you eat them any time. As I said, you'll be sick of the sight of them before we go home." He stood up and helped the ladies from the ornate chairs that surrounded the dining table. "It's busier in there than I expected for a lunchtime."

"You probably didn't spend much time in here before you moved to London. You'd have been too young."

Archie nodded. "Certainly not at this time of day. The fishermen are out early each morning, though, and so once they're back, their work's done for the day."

"I wouldn't swap with them," Henry said.

Archie smirked at his son. "Why do you think I moved south?"

Once out of the inn, Archie led the group down the shallow incline of the road towards the shoreline.

"That's Aunty Jean's house next to the smokehouse." Archie pointed to a wooden building adjoining the first cottage on the left-hand side, which sat on the edge of the beach. "Mr Stewart's parents live next door. It's quite a family business."

"What do they all do?" Connie screwed up her nose as they walked past.

"The men, and those in the other cottages, are all fishermen and once they bring the catch back, the women fillet the fish, then either pack them up for the market or prepare them for smoking."

"Is that what the smell is?"

Archie laughed. "A mixture of fish waste and smoke. You'll get used to it, eventually, but we'll keep walking to Maggie's first. I didn't speak to her last night, and it's only a little further down on the right." He knocked on the front door and when no one came to open it, he let himself in.

"Is anyone home?"

Maggie appeared from a room to the left of the hallway, a smile brightening her face, but it quickly disappeared. "I wasn't expecting to see you until tonight. Is everything all right?"

Archie rolled his eyes. "That's not much of a welcome. I didn't see much of you yesterday, and so I thought I'd make amends. Besides, I've already shown Eliza and Mrs Appleton around the village. There's little else to do."

Maggie laughed. "You're not wrong. Did you like what you saw?"

"Oh, we did." Connie clapped her hands under her chin. "It's very picturesque."

"It is on a lovely sunny day like this; it's not quite so

19

charming in the middle of winter, but I wouldn't go anywhere else. May I get you all a cup of tea?" She led the way into a kitchen, which was a similar size to her ma's but far less cluttered.

"I presume Robert's at work." Archie took a seat at the table.

Maggie was at the sink filling up the kettle, but Eliza noticed her shoulders tense.

"No, he's not. In fact, I thought it was him when you arrived. I was expecting him home an hour ago."

"Ah. Is this because he's gone to fetch his ma?"

Maggie slammed the kettle onto the range and lit it with a match before facing her guests. "Yes, it is, although why on earth she's coming, I've no idea."

"You said she wanted to see Archie."

Archie shot Eliza an icy stare. "Don't blame me."

"No, don't blame him." Maggie sat next to her brother. "It's nothing but an excuse. She's up to something ... but I can't figure out what."

Eliza twisted one corner of her mouth. "You mentioned last night that the two of you don't get along. That could be awkward."

"Don't I know it. The thing is, we'd manage well enough if she stopped treating Robert as her handyman. Since his father died, he's never here, and if he's not careful, he'll lose his job."

"How does he manage that if she lives over an hour away?"

"That's exactly the point. She stayed out there of her own accord but expects Robert to be at her beck and call and it can't go on."

"Don't upset yourself." Archie patted her hand.

"I can't help it. She's probably had him doing some work this morning while he's been there to pick her up. He should be back by now. The coal won't deliver itself and he has a big round. It's just fortunate for him it's summer and people aren't desperate for deliveries."

"Where are the girls?" Archie asked, as if trying to change the subject.

"They're outside, doing the laundry. We've had to borrow a bed from next door and by the time they'd brought it in here and set it up, they were running late. Robert should have been here to help. I just don't understand; she never normally visits. Why now…?"

Maggie stared into space as two young women with neatly tied back ginger hair disturbed the silence.

"Ma, what's the matter? Aren't you taking the kettle off the stove?"

"Goodness, yes, thank you." Maggie jumped up and grabbed a cloth before indicating towards her daughters. "This is Flora and Caitlin. Girls, this is Uncle Archie and his family: Cousin Henry, Aunt Eliza and her companion Mrs Appleton."

"Here, let me do that." The taller of the two, Flora, took the tea towel from her mother and picked the kettle up. "You sit down before you do any damage."

"It's all of your own making." Caitlin rummaged in a cupboard and pulled out a cake tin. "Grandma isn't so bad, and look at it this way, if she's staying here for a few weeks, Pa won't need to call on her. We should use this as a chance to get her to move back here."

Maggie's already pale face lost all trace of colour. "I don't know what would be worse, having her on the doorstep or Pa travelling over there all the time. She'd never leave us alone..."

Archie put a hand on his sister's. "I'm sure she can't be that bad. Just take a few deep breaths and have a cup of tea."

The tea hadn't been poured for more than a minute when the sound of horses' hooves outside the kitchen window had Maggie on her feet.

"They're here. Right–" she instinctively reached up to tidy her hair and took a deep breath "–just act normally."

Eliza pushed her chair from the table. "Shall we leave to give you time to settle her in?"

"Gracious, no, please stay where you are. It might be for the best ... and she wants to see Archie, apparently. It'll save you coming back."

An uneasy tension settled over the room as they waited for Robert and his ma to join them. Finally, the door opened, and Robert Scott's rough voice filtered in from the hallway.

"Mind the step." A balding man with dark eyes and a moustache ushered in a slender woman with immaculately styled, light grey hair.

"I can manage, I'm not an invalid."

"No, of course not ... gosh, a welcoming party." Robert stepped forward and offered a hand to Archie. "I wasn't expecting you to be here."

Archie shook the outstretched hand before offering his seat to Mrs Scott. "Allow me."

"Oh, what a gentleman, thank you."

"Ma, this is Dr Thomson. Remember, you wanted to see him."

Despite the agitation on her face, Mrs Scott smiled. "Dr Thomson, I've been so looking forward to meeting you again."

"Not in a medical capacity, I hope. You look spritely enough."

"Oh, there's nothing wrong with me, it's just nice to see you again. Now, are you going to introduce me to your lovely family?"

Maggie refilled the kettle while Archie introduced everyone.

"Have you eaten?" Maggie asked when she turned back to her husband. "I thought you'd be home by noon so when it got to one o'clock, I decided not to wait."

"We ate before we left." Mrs Scott studied Eliza before her pale blue eyes flicked towards her daughter-in-law. "I don't have a big appetite, but who can say when I'll eat properly again."

"If the cakes are anything to go by, I'm sure you'll be well looked after." Connie glanced down at her now empty plate.

"I can't live on tea and cakes. I'm very particular, you know."

"Yes, you are." Maggie took a deep breath. "Do you want the girls to show you where you're staying?"

"Not now, we have visitors. There'll be time enough for that later. You need to tidy up in here, anyway. You wouldn't find my kitchen in this state."

Eliza glanced around the room. Except for the cups, there wasn't a thing out of place.

"I'm sorry. I won't serve tea next time you come." Maggie returned to the sink but made no attempt to wash up.

"Don't be like that." Mrs Scott's voice was abrupt. "At least when Flora and Caitlin come to stay with me, you won't have so much to do."

"What!" Maggie spun around to face her mother-in-law.

"Don't raise your voice at me. I need some help at home and what's the point of having granddaughters if they can't come and help me out from time to time?"

"And what am I supposed to do?"

Mrs Scott flicked a hand in the air. "You'll manage; you're much less particular than I am."

"Robert, are you just going to sit there while she takes our daughters away?" Maggie's cheeks burned red.

"It'll only be for a few days. Isn't that right, Ma?"

"I haven't decided yet..."

Eliza glanced at Archie. "I think we called at a bad time. Why don't we leave you to settle Mrs Scott in and we'll see you later."

Archie was on his feet before she finished speaking. "Yes, we want to visit Jean, anyway. Will you be joining us this evening, Mrs Scott?"

"I couldn't tell you what I'm doing, but if there's a family gathering, then I'll be there."

"Splendid."

Henry was already by the door and held it open as they all filed out. "Good grief, what was that all about? I hope they sort themselves out before tonight or it will be a right barrel of laughs."

"Should we warn Jean about it?" Eliza asked, but Archie shook his head.

"No, don't give her anything to worry about. Hopefully, they'll be fine by this evening."

CHAPTER FOUR

Archie spotted Fraser on the beach with his brother-in-law, Mr Stewart, as they approached Jean's house. Their sons were with them, examining several lengths of fishing net that stretched out across the pebbles.

"Are you doing the mending?" Archie asked as he joined them.

A dark-haired man with a bushy moustache straightened up to greet him. "Archie. Good to see you." Mr Stewart extended a hand. "Thankfully, we had a big haul this morning, but it's done a bit of damage."

"I notice Fraser isn't helping you."

Fraser leaned against the side of a small fishing boat as he watched Rabbie and Callum help their cousins. "I'm giving them moral support."

"I like your style." Archie laughed before turning around to introduce the family.

"You are coming tonight, aren't you?" Mr Stewart's weathered face creased into a frown.

"Yes, of course. I just thought we'd get the introductions over with first."

Mr Stewart put a hand to his chest. "Thank goodness for that. Jean would be beside herself if you weren't. She's been preparing all morning."

"Do you think we ought to disturb her then?" Eliza asked.

"Och, you'll be fine. It's all done now. Go on in and we'll follow you. It'll prompt her to put the kettle on."

Fraser pushed himself away from the boat. "I'll come in with you; all this sea air's made me hungry."

Archie rolled his eyes. "What an excuse. You get plenty of sea air in Glasgow, especially with working at the shipyard."

"Ah, but this is different. It's not accompanied by the smell of fish, for one thing."

Archie raised an eyebrow. "That makes you hungry? It has the opposite effect on the rest of us."

"It certainly does." Eliza covered her nose with a handkerchief and followed them into the house, but if the air smelt of fish outside, it was nothing to what greeted them as they went indoors.

"Are you still doing the smoking?" Archie smiled as he waited for his sister to turn around.

"You're here!" Jean threw her arms around him. "I cooled the smoker down an hour ago, hoping the smell would have faded, but if it hasn't, I'll open the doors and windows. You didn't use to complain."

Archie laughed. "That was when I knew no better." He introduced the family before they went into the living room.

"Have a seat and I'll make us a pot of tea. It isn't as bad in here as in the kitchen." Jean pushed the window open as wide as she could. "I imagine the others will be stopping now, too. I hope they haven't much left to do. They need to get themselves cleaned up by five o'clock ready for tonight."

"We're almost done." Mr Stewart walked in to hear the end of Jean's sentence. "Another half an hour should do it."

"Well, we won't keep you," Eliza said. "You really needn't make more tea; we've just had one with Maggie."

"Nonsense. What would you think of me?"

"Let us help you then."

Eliza and Connie joined Jean in the kitchen as she busied herself with the kettle.

"How was Maggie when you saw her?" Jean asked. "She's not been herself these last few days. Worrying about Mrs Scott's visit, I'd say."

"She was rather unsettled when we got there and didn't improve when Mrs Scott arrived."

"Ah, she's here, is she? That should make tonight interesting. Our Maggie had better behave herself." With the kettle on the stove, Jean found a selection of cakes.

"Please don't go to any trouble. A cup of tea will be fine."

"I'm sure the men won't turn them down, not my lot at any rate."

"Yes, of course." Eliza moved to the window while Jean laid out the tray. "My goodness, there's Maggie and Mrs Scott walking towards the inn. They even seem to be speaking to each other. When we left, I'd have sworn Maggie was about to lose her temper."

Jean followed her gaze. "Robert's probably calmed things down."

"Hmm, maybe."

"I imagine they'll be going to the shop. It's further up the road, past The Coach House, near the headland."

27

"They put a shop at the top of the hill?" Connie put a hand to her mouth when she realised she'd spoken out loud but Jean only laughed.

"It's in the centre of the village. There are houses over the other side, too. It's a smashing view from up there. I hope you're used to hills; you'll be walking up there soon enough."

"Mrs Scott doesn't seem to be having much trouble and so I'm sure we'll be fine." Eliza waited until the two women disappeared and then picked up the platter of cakes. "Shall we go through?"

Mr Stewart, Archie and Fraser were in one corner of the room near the window, while Henry stood with his cousins in the other.

"Aren't you talking to each other?" Jean put the tray down on a writing desk alongside the fireplace.

"It makes a change to have different company," Mr Stewart said.

"I thought we might have seen you last night at Ma's house." Archie walked to the tray and helped himself to a slice of shortbread.

Jean shook her head. "And get in the way of you and Ma? I don't think so. She sees enough of me." She lowered her voice as she leaned over to Eliza. "How was she with you?"

Eliza grimaced. "We're still speaking to each other ... I think."

Jean released a sigh. "Oh good. I hoped you hadn't fallen out already given that you're all here tonight."

"That did cross my mind." Eliza took a seat next to Connie on the settee opposite the fire. "Do you have many coming later?"

"Only family. That's enough with everyone being here. And don't look so worried; Ma won't trouble you."

"I hope not."

With the tea and cakes finished, Archie and Henry followed Mr Stewart outside, while Eliza and Connie helped Jean with the tidying up.

"That was lovely, thank you." Eliza dried the last plate and passed it to Connie, who put it back on the dresser. "We'd better be going, though, it's nearly half past three and I imagine you want some time to sort yourself out."

"Oh, don't worry about me, I'm on top of everything. I just need to bring the fish in from the smoker, but they can wait." Jean walked them to the door. "I'm glad you called, it's nice to see you again. It's such a shame you're so far away."

"I know, but despite the improvements in the railways, the journey doesn't get any better."

Connie rolled her eyes at Jean. "Don't start her on that again."

Eliza sighed. "Don't worry, I won't say another word, but perhaps we should play host to you next time. If ever you'd like to come down to London..."

"Oh, I'm not sure about that." Jean stepped outside to where Archie, Henry and Fraser were staring at what now looked like a jumble of nets. "London's not for the likes of us."

Eliza watched as the men tried to straighten out the mess before them. "It will take them until the morning to unravel that lot again!"

Jean crossed her arms over her chest. "They know what they're doing. They'll be folded up nicely by the time you're back."

With a final farewell, Eliza and Connie collected Archie and Henry and made their way back to The Coach House.

"It'll be nice to sit in the lounge and read my book," Eliza said. "I've not had a minute since we got off the train."

"Well, don't get too engrossed. We have to be back by half past five."

"That still gives us over an hour. You and Henry can go for a walk if you want."

"No, I'd rather just sit and read the paper."

"Can I go back to the beach then?" Henry asked.

Eliza glanced at Archie. "I don't see why not, as long as you're not late back."

With Henry disappearing, they continued to The Coach House, but as they reached the door, they were stopped by the sound of voices coming from further up the hill.

"Is that Maggie and Mr Scott?" Eliza glanced at Archie. "They look like they're arguing."

"It could be about Mrs Scott," Connie said.

Archie stared at them. "You go in without me; I'll be back in a minute."

"And miss all the fun? I don't think so." Eliza grinned at Connie. "We can just as easily wait here."

Archie scowled at her. "You shouldn't be taking delight in other people's misfortune."

"No, you're right." She waited for Archie to be out of earshot before grinning at Connie. "It does liven the place up, though. I wonder what's going on." Eliza edged forward. "Should we go and find out?"

They hadn't caught Archie up before he and Maggie turned and left Mr Scott staring out to sea.

"What's the matter?" Eliza asked.

"His ma, that's what's the matter." Maggie's face was scarlet as she continued walking.

"But she's not here."

"Exactly! And she should be." Maggie spun around and pointed up the hill. "I left her on the bench just beyond the shop and when I went back to get her, she'd disappeared. We've been home, and she isn't there, and we've no idea where else she could be."

Robert's face was like thunder as he joined them. "Why Maggie left her alone, I'll never know."

"I've told you, she wanted me to. She said she was meeting someone, and I was only to go back when I'd been in the shop for at least fifteen minutes. I didn't even *need* anything, but she insisted."

"Well, who was she meeting?" A vein throbbed in Robert's neck.

"I don't know. Either she didn't tell me, or I wasn't listening."

"Knowing you, you weren't listening. Try to remember."

Maggie's eyes implored Archie. "Tell him I can't remember something I didn't know in the first place."

Eliza stepped forward. "If she said she was meeting someone, perhaps they've invited her in for tea and she's not noticed the time. There must be a perfectly simple explanation."

Robert continued to glare at Maggie. "You'd better be right."

"I'm sure she is." Archie linked Eliza's arm through his. "From what I remember, Mrs Scott lived here for a long time before she moved away. She'll have friends she won't have seen for years and she's probably catching up with

31

someone. Why don't you go home. She can find her own way around."

Robert nodded and took Maggie's arm as they joined them in walking back to the inn. They made the short journey to the inn in silence before saying their farewells.

"What a performance." Archie paused outside the inn as he watched his sister and brother-in-law continue their journey home. "I've never seen Maggie like that. Let's hope Mrs Scott returns before we get to Jean's tonight."

CHAPTER FIVE

The sun was on their backs as Eliza and Archie walked to the Stewarts' house with Connie and Henry later that evening.

"I expect you to stay here tonight," Eliza said to Henry. "No sneaking back to The Coach House."

Henry's shoulders sank. "But it's easier to talk there and there'll be five of us. I hardly spoke to Niall and Ross earlier, with them mending the nets."

"Flora and Caitlin won't be able to go out and so it's only manners for you all to stay together. Why should they get left behind?"

"We can't take girls with us."

Eliza let out an exasperated gasp. "Precisely. That's why you shouldn't be so rude as to ignore them. I'm sure you could all slip out onto the beach if you don't want to stay indoors."

Henry tutted. "I suppose so, but what if the others want to go?"

"You tell them what I've just told you."

Henry hung back as Eliza and Connie went inside.

"Either I'm getting used to the smell or leaving the windows open did the trick," Connie said. "It's not as bad as it was earlier."

"Thankfully! Let's hope they have some aromatic punch to sniff if the need arises."

Connie chuckled, but her laugh faltered when she saw Maggie, her eyes red.

"A-are you all right?"

"No, I'm not. That damn woman hasn't had the common decency to come home yet. I'd swear she does it on purpose just to cause trouble."

"Where's Mr Scott?" Eliza glanced around the room.

"He can't settle. He walked me over here, but he's gone up to the headland to look for her again. He's still blaming me for not listening to what she said."

"I'm sorry." Eliza nodded to the punch in Maggie's hand. "Is there any gin in it?"

Maggie emptied her glass. "Not enough."

"Let me get you another."

Maggie shook her head. "Jean's already told me I've had too many. I'll help myself to another when she's not looking. I'll see you later."

Eliza moved over to the silver punchbowl where Jean was ladling lemon-coloured liquid into the small cups arranged around the base. She handed one each to Eliza and Connie.

"A little treat," Jean said. "Just don't lose your cup in case you want another one."

"One will be quite enough for me," Connie said. "Alcohol has a habit of making me dizzy."

"Ooh, you'd better take care then, there's rather a lot of gin in it."

Connie immediately pulled the cup away from her lips. "I will, thank you."

Jean let her eyes wander around her guests. "I think you know everyone. Fraser's just gone up the road to collect Ma and Pa. He won't be long."

Eliza took a gulp from her drink. "You should have said, they could have walked with us."

"I'm sure they could, but she wanted Fraser to walk her down. You know what she's like. Set in her ways."

And she couldn't bring herself to spend any time with me!

Jean pointed to Maggie, who was now at the opposite side of the room with Flora and Caitlin. "We need to keep an eye on her. Apparently, Mrs Scott hasn't turned up yet and I don't trust her not to drink too much punch and argue with Robert. She's already had two."

"She seemed all right when we arrived." Eliza took another sip of the drink that tasted of nothing but lemonade. "She's just angry that Mrs Scott deliberately stayed out so late."

"That's as maybe, but would you mind standing by the bowl to make sure she doesn't help herself to any more. I want to get the kippers ready for when Ma and Pa arrive."

"I'm not sure we can..."

"Of course you can. Tell her I said so." Without another word, Jean disappeared, leaving Eliza holding the ladle.

Connie put her nose to the cup. "Is it very strong?"

"No, not at all, it's mainly lemonade and some berries from the hedgerows."

"So, it won't make me dizzy?"

Eliza laughed. "You could drink the whole bowl and it would have no effect on you."

Connie was about to respond when the chattering that had filled the room faded.

"Here we are." Fraser stepped into the room with Mr and Mrs Thomson. "It looks like a full house and so I'd say the party can start."

"Except for Robert and his ma." Maggie's voice was bitter.

Fraser released his ma's arm and went over to Maggie. "Has she not turned up? We'll send a search party out for her tomorrow if there's still no sign of her."

"That's where Robert is now. We've another couple of hours' daylight yet."

"I hope we're not going to wait for them." Mrs Thomson's voice filled the room. "Where's Jean?"

"She's just in the kitchen preparing the kippers. May I get you a drink?" Eliza picked up the ladle, but her hand stopped short of the cups when her mother-in-law glared at her.

"Who put you in charge of that?"

"J-Jean did. She asked me to watch over it while she's busy. Would you like some?"

"Fraser will pour mine. I'll take a seat." Eliza watched the old woman walk towards the fire before she handed the ladle to Fraser and turned her attention to her father-in-law.

"What would you like, Mr Thomson?"

"A large Scotch."

"Oh, I'm sorry. Jean didn't leave any of that."

"She wouldn't have, but that husband of hers will have some, somewhere. Where is he?"

Eliza scanned the room. "Now you mention it, I've not seen him this evening. He may be outside."

Without a word, Mr Thomson left, prompting a deep sigh from Eliza.

"I don't know what I have to do for them to be civil to me."

Connie nodded. "It is strange given Dr Thomson thought they'd be pleased with you for suggesting the visit."

"Oh, they're better than they were. So far, they've only been rude, last time they were downright nasty."

Connie sighed. "All because you made Dr Thomson stay in London?"

"Apparently so." Eliza helped herself to another glass of punch. "Have you tried this yet? I would if I were you. Despite the lack of gin, it's rather pleasant and the kippers will be here in a minute."

As the night drew in, most of the family congregated around the fireplace to recount folklore of old. Eliza had listened out of politeness, but once the ghost stories began, she pulled Connie to one side. "Where did Henry get to, did you notice?"

Connie shook her head. "I can't say I did. He might be on the beach like you suggested."

"Shall we go and see?" Eliza led the way to the back door. "You know, there are times I wish I was a young boy, all the freedom he has."

"We have more than most."

"I know, but it's not the same, is it?"

The back door was open when they reached it and they stepped out onto a sand-covered terrace.

"It is lovely out here and smells so fresh after being indoors. We should have come out earlier to take in the view." Eliza edged forward towards the beach. "There they all are."

She pointed over to their right. "How lovely to see everyone with a smile on their faces. I tell you, between Archie's mother and Maggie, tonight was an effort."

"It's done now, perhaps tomorrow we can walk to the other side of the village and get away for a few hours."

"Yes, that would be nice." Eliza leaned on the fence that separated the house from the beach and turned to face the headland, which now stood on their right. "Look at the houses up there. Imagine the views they must have. They're big, too. I suppose some important people live up there."

In the fading light, Connie stepped to Eliza's side but immediately straightened up and pointed to the base of the headland. "What's that over there?"

Eliza took another step forward. "I don't know, some material, perhaps, or could it be some nets that have been washed up?"

"Here you are. I wondered where you'd gone."

Eliza turned as Archie and Mr Stewart joined them.

"We were just taking a breath of air before the light faded, but we've spotted that." Eliza's brow furrowed as she pointed to the object. "What do you think it is? It's difficult to see in this light."

Mr Stewart leaned over the fence. "I'd say something's come off one of the boats, some tarpaulin or something."

"That's what I thought when I first saw it, but now I'm not so sure." A shiver ran down Eliza's spine. "You don't think it could be a body, do you?"

Archie chuckled and patted her hand. "Oh, my dear, let's not have any of that. We're in St Giles now, not London. You don't find dead bodies here."

Eliza looked back at the shape. "Should we go and check?"

"You can't go out there now." Mr Stewart's face was stern. "It's high tide shortly; you wouldn't get there and back before the sea cut you off."

"But if it's a body…"

"If it's a body, it will be dead, and you'll be joining it if you insist on this nonsense. It's folly to cross the beach with the tide so high."

"But what about Mrs Scott? Maybe there's a more sinister reason why she didn't return to Maggie's."

Archie shook his head. "How much punch have you had? Your imagination's even more vivid than usual. I'm sure Mr Stewart can recognise a piece of tarpaulin when he sees one."

"I only had a couple of glasses … and there wasn't much gin in it."

Mr Stewart ushered them back indoors. "I'll check as soon as I get back in the morning; don't you worry yourself about it."

Eliza stopped. "What time will that be?"

"About eight o'clock. By the time you wake up, you'll wonder what all the fuss was about. Now, if you'll excuse me, I need to go to bed. The boat needs to be on the water by four o'clock in the morning."

"Is everything all right?" Jean asked as they all traipsed back through the kitchen.

"There's something at the base of the headland and I wondered if…"

"That's enough, Eliza." Archie took her arm and pulled her to one side. "There's no point alarming anyone else. I'll come down to the beach tomorrow, as well, and if it is more than a piece of tarpaulin, I promise I'll ride over to St Andrews for the police."

"The police!" Jean put her hands to her face.

Archie sighed. "You weren't supposed to be listening."

Mr Stewart put an arm around his wife's shoulders. "There won't be any need for them. Mrs Thomson's clearly had too much to drink."

Eliza was about to object, but suddenly changed her mind. If it got her out of here, it was a price worth paying. "Yes, I'm sorry, we'd better go. We can call for Henry on the way out."

Once they'd indicated to Henry they were leaving, they started walking back to the inn.

"Did you really agree with Mr Stewart when he said it was tarpaulin?" Eliza asked Archie as they approached his parents' house.

"Well, the man makes his livelihood from the sea; he should know what he's looking at."

"You have to admit, though, the outline did resemble a body."

Eliza turned at the sound of footsteps running up behind them and smiled at Henry.

"You left rather suddenly."

"Your mother's under the impression she saw a dead body on the beach and so we decided it was time for her to have a lie down and sleep off the gin."

Eliza stopped, exhaling loudly. "Will you stop saying that? I've had no more to drink than anyone else. Besides, Connie hardly touched a drop, and she agrees with me. Don't you, Connie?"

"Well, yes, you have a point. It was difficult to tell."

"Will we be doing some sleuthing tomorrow then?" Henry's eyes glistened in the moonlight.

"No, we will not." Archie ushered them all into the inn. "I'll go to the beach in the morning and no doubt I'll be back in time for breakfast to give you a full report."

CHAPTER SIX

H enry was sitting at the breakfast table the next morning when Eliza and Connie arrived downstairs.

"Isn't your father back yet?"

Henry shook his head. "I've not seen him."

Eliza's brow furrowed. "That's strange. He left before seven this morning and it's nearly nine now." She reached for Connie's hand. "Do you think he's found a body?"

Connie gulped. "He may have done. If it was only a piece of tarpaulin, he'd be at the table waiting for us, like he promised."

"Unless he's met someone? He could be talking," Henry suggested.

Eliza studied her son. "He's still been gone a long time."

Henry pushed back his chair. "I'll walk down and find out what's happening."

"Not on your own, you won't, wait for us." Eliza jumped up, thankful she was already wearing her hat. "It's a good job we came prepared. We'll have something to eat later."

Connie dropped the piece of toast she had just taken from

the rack on the table and followed Eliza outside. "Where are we going?"

"Down to the beach." Eliza hitched up the front of her skirt. "I knew we were looking at a body last night. Why didn't he come and tell us?"

"I imagine he's rather preoccupied if it is. We'd better get a move on if we don't want to miss anything." Henry led the way to the Stewarts' house and onto the beach before doubling back towards the headland.

"There's a lot of activity." Connie pointed to a handful of people dotted around the rocks.

"And there's Archie. It looks like the police are here, too."

"And Aunty Maggie and Mr Scott."

Despite her lungs protesting, Eliza broke into a run, reaching Archie first. "What's going on?"

Archie gestured to the piece of tarpaulin lying by his feet. "Mrs Scott."

"Oh, goodness." Eliza's stomach somersaulted, and she glanced across to Maggie and Mr Scott. "Did she drown?"

Archie shook his head and turned his back on the rest of the group. "She fell from the headland."

Eliza's eyes narrowed as she stared from the body to the steep incline of the rock. "Fell? Is this where you found her?"

"Yes, she was here when I arrived, but Maggie and Mr Scott were already here. I don't think they slept much last night."

"And did you leave them here while you fetched the police?"

"What else could I do? I wasn't gone long though; no more than an hour. Fortunately, with it being so early, they weren't busy with anything and came straight back with me."

Eliza wandered towards the cliff face, beckoning the others to follow her. "Don't you think she's too far away from the drop for it to be a simple fall?"

Archie strained his neck to look upwards. "I did wonder, but the officers said the tide probably moved her when it was going out."

Eliza surveyed the scene before studying the body once more. "Can I see it?"

"No, you can't. This is a police investigation; you can't disturb the evidence."

"It may have been disturbed already."

"Maybe it has, but the body didn't move between me leaving here and arriving back with the police. The only thing Mr Scott did was straighten the tarpaulin over her."

Eliza's eyes narrowed. "Does Mr Stewart know about this?"

"No, he doesn't, he's still out at sea; it appears they've been delayed. Maggie's spoken to Jean, but she wouldn't come out. She's not as interested in dead bodies as you."

Eliza opened her mouth to respond but closed it again when the police sergeant and his young constable joined them.

"Right, we'll be off then, Dr Thomson. Can I leave you to watch over the body while we call the mortuary and get them to collect it? I'll tell them they need to be here before the tide comes back in."

"What time will that be?"

"High tide's due at around midday, that's why we need to hurry. If no one arrives by eleven o'clock, get yourselves off the beach before you're trapped. The body won't go far."

"Very well." Archie nodded. "I'll call into the station later this afternoon with the death certificate and a statement."

"Very good." The sergeant widened his arms to usher Eliza and Connie from the scene. "If you wouldn't mind walking with us, this is no place for ladies."

"Actually, Officer, I'd like a quick word with my husband. We'll follow you."

The sergeant looked to Archie, who nodded. "I'll take care of them."

"Very well. Good day to you all."

The group watched the officers leave.

"That was very restrained of you," Connie said when they were out of earshot.

"It was, wasn't it? I didn't know I had it in me." Eliza chuckled. "Now may we look at the body?"

"No! I've told you."

Eliza's shoulders sagged. "All right, but wouldn't it be educational to take Henry through the wounds? It might help him with his studies."

Henry's eyes sparkled. "I was thinking the same thing."

"Well..." Archie gave Eliza a sideways glance. "I suppose so."

"Excellent. In that case, there'll be no harm if Connie and I watch, will there?"

Archie scowled at her. "Very well, but do it discreetly. I don't want to upset Mr Scott any further."

Eliza looked around. "Where is he?"

"It looks like he's gone although Maggie's still here." Connie indicated to one of the large rocks at the base of the headland where Maggie sat in deep contemplation.

"He was rather upset," Archie said. "Perhaps he just wanted to be alone."

"Poor thing. It must be such a shock." Connie bowed her head as Eliza watched Archie and Henry pull the tarpaulin away from Mrs Scott's torso.

"How long has she been dead?" Eliza asked.

"When I arrived this morning, the body was still stiff but the muscles are loosening again and so I'd say at least twelve hours although probably longer."

"How much longer?"

Archie shrugged. "Basically, it could be any time between when she disappeared and about eight or nine o'clock last night."

"Which would fit with us seeing the body last night."

Henry stooped down by Mrs Scott's head. "There are several nasty cuts that would have been made by the rocks when she fell."

"But are they enough to have killed her?" Eliza asked. "The drop isn't that high."

"It's high enough. The rocks down here are quite rugged." Archie said.

Eliza stared at the body before she bent down beside Henry. "What's this?"

"Don't touch anything." Archie pulled her up, but as he did, Eliza caught hold of a scarf. It came away easily.

"Do the rocks explain that?" She pointed to several dark marks around Mrs Scott's neck.

Henry raised an eyebrow to his father. "Did you miss that?"

Archie coughed to clear his throat. "That wasn't there earlier. It must have developed as the body's lain here."

"Could it mean someone wanted to make sure she was dead after she'd fallen?"

Archie bobbed his head from side to side. "Not necessarily. She could have been strangled first..."

"And then thrown from the headland? That would explain why she's so far from the cliff face." Eliza stood up to re-examine the scene.

"It's as well she wasn't thrown any further." Connie stared down at the seaweed less than two feet from them. "The body would have been washed away if she was, and you may never have found her."

"Oh my goodness, Connie, you're right. Maybe that was the plan. Someone wanted her dead and tried to fling the body out to sea in the hope it wouldn't come back."

"Now you're getting carried away." Archie replaced the cover over Mrs Scott's head. "We don't know for certain that this is where she fell."

"But based on the line made by the seaweed, one thing we can say is, it wasn't moved by the sea. That clearly shows how high the tide came up the beach and it didn't come this far. Besides, her clothes are dry."

"But why would anyone want to murder Mrs Scott?" Connie asked.

"Why indeed?" Eliza's eyes twinkled. "Shall we have a word with Maggie?"

Maggie looked up as they joined her, the rims of her eyes red.

"How are you feeling?" Eliza found a place to sit on a nearby rock.

"Numb. I mean, what was she doing up there to be able to fall?"

"Isn't the edge of the headland close to the bench where you left her?"

"Well, yes, but not so close that she would have fallen if she'd stayed where she was."

"How's Mr Scott taking it?" Archie asked.

Maggie buried her face in her hands. "He blames me. Says that if I hadn't left her..."

"It's not your fault. You said she wanted you to leave her."

"She did."

Eliza gazed at the cliff beside them. "So, what can you tell us about the events of yesterday afternoon? What did you do once you left Mrs Scott?"

Maggie wiped her eyes on her handkerchief. "We walked up to the top of the headland. I thought we were going to the shop, but she told me she was meeting somebody by the bench. I swear she didn't tell me who, but Robert won't believe me."

"Did she walk to the bench herself?"

"No, I was with her. The road that runs up there is on quite an incline and so I got her settled before I walked back to the shop."

"And how long did you stay there?"

Maggie shrugged. "I don't know exactly, twenty to twenty-five minutes. It was empty and so I stayed to talk to Mrs Baker – she's the shopkeeper's wife."

"Was Mr Baker in?"

"No, he'd gone into St Andrews to pick up some stock. That's why she was happy to talk. She couldn't have stood talking for so long if he'd been around."

"Can you see the bench from the shop?" Henry asked.

"No, there's a bend in the road just past the church."

"But if she'd left to walk back to the village, would you have seen her?" Eliza asked.

Maggie hesitated. "Not necessarily."

"The window at the front of the shop has shelves in it to display the goods," Archie explained.

"And I had my back to the door. It didn't occur to me she might disappear."

Eliza nodded. "So basically, once you were in the shop, Mrs Scott could have gone anywhere?"

"I suppose she could."

Eliza tapped a finger on her lips. "We were at Jean's house and saw you and Mrs Scott walking towards the headland. That would have been about two o'clock. How long did it take you to get there?"

"Not long, five minutes or so."

"So, you left her at about five past two; what time did you go back?"

Maggie puffed out her cheeks. "As I say, it was about twenty minutes, maybe a bit longer. In fact, yes, that's right because I heard the church clock ring for half past two as I was searching the headland for her."

Eliza bit down on her lip. "Can anyone confirm that?"

"What? That I went back to the bench."

"No, that you were on the headland when the bells rang ... and that Mrs Scott had disappeared by then."

"Well ... erm ... I couldn't say. Mrs Baker knows when I left her, but, no, I don't think I saw anyone else."

"So, what did you do once you realised she was missing?"

Archie shot Eliza a glance.

"My heart sank, I can tell you." Maggie wiped her eyes

again. "I wanted to be back for Jean's party, and I was worried she'd make us late."

"Did you call for her?"

A frown crossed Maggie's face. "No, not really. As soon as I saw that she wasn't on the bench, I started looking for her. I even walked down the road towards St Andrews until I got to the end of the houses, which is when I turned around. That's when I met Robert and you saw us shortly afterwards."

Eliza thought back to the previous afternoon. "If I remember rightly, that was at about half past three. So, over an hour since you'd last seen Mrs Scott and we only have Mrs Baker to say you stayed in the shop until about twenty-five past two."

Maggie's features darkened. "What are you suggesting?"

"I'm not suggesting anything, I'm just going through what the police are likely to ask."

"I've already spoken to them and they didn't ask anything of the sort."

Eliza studied her. "They didn't?"

"Why would they? Ma had obvious gone too close to the edge and slipped."

Eliza looked back to the body not ten feet from them. "Did you move the body when you found it this morning?"

Maggie shuddered. "I did not. Archie's the only person who's touched it."

Eliza chewed on her lip as she studied the rocks. "The thing is, if Mrs Scott had fallen, you'd expect the body to be closer to the rocks; but ... well, it's nearly twenty feet away."

Maggie shrugged. "It must have hit something and bounced over here."

Eliza glanced at Archie, who took a seat beside his sister.

"The problem is, Mags, Mrs Scott has marks around her neck that suggests she was strangled before she ended up down here."

Maggie's face turned white as her mouth opened and closed without her speaking.

Archie took her hands. "It looks as if she was murdered and then her body thrown onto the beach by someone hoping it would be carried out to sea."

"But who'd do that?"

"That's what we'd like you to think about..."

"Dr Thomson?"

Everyone turned to see two men approaching, their black robes suggesting they'd arrived to take the body away.

Archie stood up. "It's just over here."

Eliza watched as they prepared the body for removal until, eventually, they carried it away on a stretcher. "We'd better be going too, if we don't want to get trapped by the tide."

"I need to wait for Robert." Maggie glanced further along the beach.

"Where did he go?" Archie asked as he rejoined them. "I'll see if I can find him."

"He needed time on his own; he could be anywhere."

Archie took his sister's arm. "That's understandable. His ma's just been found dead." He urged her to go with them to the road.

"I suppose..."

"Come on, let's get you home. I'm sure he'll be able to make his own way back."

Eliza walked on Maggie's other side. "Once we've got you

settled, we'll go up to the headland and see if we can find any clues about who could have done such a thing."

Maggie's blue eyes widened. "You really think she was murdered?"

Eliza nodded. "I'm afraid so."

"Well, I'm coming with you. If there's anything to find, I want to know about it."

CHAPTER SEVEN

The walk up the headland was steeper than Eliza expected, and both she and Connie gasped for air as they reached the bench on the top. Eliza perched herself on the seat before twisting around to study the surroundings.

"I must say, it is a splendid view, although I imagine the bench isn't just here for sight-seeing."

"You're not wrong there." Maggie sat beside her. "It's a very important stopping place when you've just walked up that hill."

"There's not a lot here, though, is there?"

"What precisely are you looking for?" Archie asked.

Eliza shrugged. "I don't know. Nothing in particular."

"She'll only know when she sees it." Connie nodded knowingly. "She does it all the time."

Maggie frowned. "You've done this before?"

A wry smile crossed Eliza's lips. "Once or twice." She stood up, distracted by the surrounding properties.

"More than that, and she's very good at it." Connie had the tone of a proud mother. "The last time we found a body..."

"Connie ... please. Can we concentrate on this?"

Archie grimaced at his sister. "She's got the bit between her teeth now. There'll be no talking to her about anything else until she's worked out what happened."

Maggie's eyes were wide. "Can't you stop her?"

Archie laughed. "It's more than my life's worth. I did try in the early days, but I've learned it's easier to let her get on with it."

"I am standing next to you." Eliza scowled at her husband before heading back down the hill.

"We're not going already, are we?" Connie hurried after her. "It wasn't worth walking up here for that."

"No, I just want a quick word with Mrs Baker. She's the shopkeeper's wife, isn't she?"

"Is this to check up on me?" Maggie's voice was raised. "Shall I come with you?"

"No, we'll be fine." Eliza waved as she continued walking.

"It would be better if you stay where you are." Archie's voice was reassuring.

"I'll go with them." Henry ran the few yards to his mother's right-hand side. "Are you checking Aunty Maggie's alibi? Don't you believe she was in the shop?"

"I'm certainly hoping she was." Eliza's heart was pounding by the time she opened the shop door and came face to face with a plump woman in her mid-fifties standing behind a wooden counter. "Mrs Baker?"

"Aye." She smoothed her hands down the front of her floral apron. "And you are?"

Eliza extended her hand. "Eliza Thomson, wife of Dr Thomson, brother of Mrs Maggie Scott. This is my son Henry and companion, Mrs Appleton."

"Oh, that's all right then. You can never be too careful with strangers around. What may I do for you?"

Eliza had already run through the conversation in her head. "I understand Maggie Scott spent some time here yesterday afternoon. Can you give me an idea of how long she stayed?"

Mrs Baker's eyes narrowed. "Why? Is that husband of hers checking up on her? He's no room to talk, going off to Cupar as often as he does..."

"No, forgive me, it's nothing like that. There's just been a bit of an accident and we need to check..."

"An accident!" Eliza had Mrs Baker's full attention now. "What's happened?"

Do I tell her? I imagine it will be all around the village within an hour if I do.

"Well?"

"Well, if you wouldn't mind keeping it to yourself..."

"Oh, you can count on me. I won't say a word." Mrs Baker leaned over the desk, her eyes flashing with excitement.

Eliza gulped. "All right, it's Maggie Scott's mother-in-law, Mrs Scott senior. We believe she may have been murdered, and..."

"Murdered!"

Eliza hoped there was no one walking outside the shop as Mrs Baker shrieked.

"Please, Mrs Baker, keep it to yourself. As far as we're aware, Maggie Scott was the last person to see her alive, and we'd like to confirm when she arrived and when she left the shop."

"Well, now then, let me think. We'd not long since

opened after lunch and so it would have been shortly after two o'clock when she got here, possibly five past."

"And she stayed to talk?"

"Oh, she did. We had a right old natter. Maggie was in no hurry because Mrs Scott had arranged to meet someone and so she'd left her on the bench outside."

Eliza eyed the full boxes of vegetables lined up in front of the counter. "How long would you say she was here?"

"Now, that's tricky, you know how time flies. Twenty minutes, maybe twenty-five, I'd say."

"You must have had a lot to talk about."

Mrs Baker lowered her voice. "She was having a bit of a moan, if I'm being honest. Mr Scott's ma had only just arrived, and she was already wishing she'd hurry up and leave again."

"She said that?" Eliza raised an eyebrow.

"Oh, don't take it the wrong way. I didn't mean she was planning to get rid of her. Heaven forbid. She wouldn't do anything like that, she was just letting off steam."

"And that was all?"

"I was sympathising with her, of course. Told her she was welcome up here whenever she wanted to get away for half an hour."

Eliza smiled. "I'm sure that would have delighted her. Is there anything else you can think of that may help us?"

Mrs Baker put a finger to her lips. "Now then, there is. After Maggie left, there was a stranger hanging around outside the church."

"A stranger?" Eliza and Connie spoke in unison.

"I couldn't say whether Maggie saw him, but he looked a shady type to me."

Eliza shook her head. "She didn't mention him."

"I'm sure she would have done if she'd seen anyone," Henry said.

Eliza pursed her lips. "You're probably right. Mrs Baker, could you give us a description of him?"

Mrs Baker glanced over both shoulders as if the man might be behind her. "A strange-looking man he was. I suppose he was of normal height, but too thin for my liking. His clothes thought so too, by the look of it. His jacket especially was much too big for him."

"What sort of age was he?"

Mrs Baker paused. "It's difficult to say but perhaps he was in his forties, possibly even his fifties; his hair was greying down the sides, but he had dark, piercing eyes."

"So, he saw you?"

"He did, and I've felt uneasy about it ever since. As soon as he realised I'd seen him, he scuttled away into the churchyard ... to hide amongst the gravestones." Mrs Baker's eyes grew wide, causing Connie to catch hold of Eliza's arm.

Henry laughed. "Don't be scared. He can't touch us in here."

"But we'll be going outside again. What if he's waiting?"

"Henry's here to protect us." Eliza removed her arm from Connie's grip and made a note on her paper. "Well, thank you, Mrs Baker. You've been very helpful."

"My pleasure. Do call again if you have any other questions."

"We will indeed. Good day."

Henry held open the door as the three of them left. "What did you make of that then? A stranger in our midst."

Eliza chuckled. "It's a good job you came with us or I'd have assumed she meant you."

"He could be the murderer." Connie's face was deadly serious.

"Possibly, although there may also be a perfectly innocent explanation for why someone Mrs Baker doesn't recognise was outside the church."

"You get the impression she knows about everything and everybody, though, don't you?" Henry paused. "She may be useful; I reckon she knows more than she thinks. Once we have a list of questions, we should come back."

"Oh, I'm sure we will."

By the time they returned to the bench, Mr Scott was with Archie and Maggie.

"May we offer our condolences, Mr Scott." Eliza paused when Mr Scott failed to acknowledge her, but Archie rested a hand on his shoulder.

"I've just been telling Mr Scott what we think happened to his mother."

"Ah, yes, it looks like it was a terrible business." Eliza paused. "We will need to ask you a few questions, just to clarify what happened, if you understand my meaning."

"No." Archie's voice was firm.

"No?" Eliza's eyebrows rose. "Don't you want to know who did such a thing?"

"Of course I do, but we need to leave it to the police. As soon as we get back to The Coach House, I'll arrange for a carriage to be prepared and drive over to St Andrews."

"And in the meantime, a stranger could be walking the streets looking for his next victim?"

"A stranger?"

Three sets of eyes stared at her.

"Yes." Eliza couldn't resist a smug grin. "According to Mrs Baker, shortly after Maggie left the shop, she saw an unknown gentleman loitering outside the church." Eliza's eyes flicked between Maggie and Mr Scott. "Did either of you notice anyone unusual yesterday, or have you seen anyone today while you've been waiting here?"

Maggie shook her head. "I don't think so, not that I've been paying much attention."

"The road's been remarkably quiet while we've been here," Archie said. "Mr Scott, did you see anyone while you were on the road?"

"I didn't walk on the road."

Eliza's eyes narrowed. "But you were on the beach ... and now you're not. How did you get here if you didn't use the road?"

"There's a footpath." Mr Scott stood up and led them to the edge of the headland where he pointed to a narrow track that turned into steps as it dropped away down the rock face.

"Why didn't Mr Stewart mention this to us last night?" Eliza's eyes narrowed. "We could have confirmed whether it was a body there and then."

Archie indicated towards the drop. "Have you seen how steep they are? It would be foolhardy to go down there in the dark."

"Even so, he could have mentioned it..."

Robert peered over the edge. "Do you think Ma could have been using the steps when she slipped, and it really was an accident?"

Archie shook his head. "I doubt it. If you stand here and look down to the beach where the body was found, there's no chance she slipped. I'm afraid Eliza was right when she suggested someone threw the body to get it as far away from the rock as possible."

Maggie stared down at the beach. "In that case, I'd say it was a man who did it. A woman couldn't throw that far."

"You're probably right." Eliza looked at Archie. "Can we go down the steps now?"

He sucked air through his teeth. "The tide looks a bit too high, perhaps later."

Eliza's shoulders slumped, but she straightened up again at the sound of Henry's voice.

"Come here." Henry pointed to the shrubs further down the footpath.

"What is it?"

"A handbag."

"A handbag?" Eliza hurried to be the first to reach it.

"There." He pointed underneath a bush to a brown crocodile-skin bag. "Aunty Maggie, could it be Mrs Scott's?"

Mr Scott spoke before his wife had a chance to look. "It's hers. She made me hold it for her yesterday as she climbed into the carriage."

Maggie nodded. "He's right. She had it with her when we walked up here. She didn't go anywhere without it."

"Well then, what's it doing here?" Eliza asked. "I doubt she accidentally dropped it."

Henry bent down to retrieve it. "Shall we see what's in it?"

"Here, let me." Eliza took it from Henry. "You keep looking in case there's anything else important."

Henry scowled at Eliza before he turned his attention back to the path. Once all eyes were on her son, Eliza unclipped the handbag and rummaged around inside. *No purse, but is this a letter? I'll read that later.* She stood with her back to the group and slipped the envelope into her own bag.

"What have you got there?" Connie peered at her.

Eliza put a finger to her lips. "I'll tell you later. Let's see what else they've found."

"Mother, here, look." Henry waved his arm to beckon her forward.

"What is it?"

"Marks in the sand."

Eliza moved Archie to one side to get a good view.

"Over there." Henry pointed to some footprints. "And it looks as if something's been dragged to the top of the steps."

"The heels of someone's shoes." Eliza spoke to herself as she pulled away from the group to stare out at the beach below. "If this is where she was thrown from, the murderer must have been strong."

"We'd better go down the steps to see if we can find anything else." Henry turned to leave.

"No." Archie grabbed his son's arm. "The tide's too dangerous. Let's get something to eat and by the time we've finished, it should be safe. We can take a more thorough look, then."

Henry nodded. "Come on, then."

"I can't go into an inn today." Mr Scott stepped away from Archie and took hold of Maggie's hand. "And neither can you."

"Robert, stop." Maggie pulled away. "I know you're upset, but we need to know what happened. You go home and I'll follow you."

Mr Scott's eyes narrowed as he glared at his wife.

"I'll take care of her." Archie put a hand on Maggie's shoulder. "I promise."

With a loud sigh, Mr Scott took his ma's handbag from Eliza and disappeared towards the road.

"Thank you." Maggie's eyes were moist as she looked at Archie. "I know I should be with him, but I'm just not up to it at the moment."

"Will the girls be at home?"

"They will, they'll see to him."

"Well, you're very welcome to join us." Archie pulled his sister's hand through the link in his arm and started towards the road. They hadn't gone far when Eliza groaned.

"Going to the inn means we'll have to walk up that hill again later!"

Archie rolled his eyes. "That should be the least of your worries, but if you'd rather not, you can wait here for us and we'll bring you a slice of bread and butter."

Eliza's stomach grumbled and she remembered they'd missed breakfast that morning. "While you eat that apple pie I spotted in the dining room earlier? I don't think so. Besides, it will give me a chance to read the letter I found."

"What letter?"

A smile brightened Eliza's face. "You'll have to wait and see."

CHAPTER EIGHT

Eliza breathed in deeply when a bowl of soup was placed in front of her. It might be more fish, but she didn't care, especially not when she smelled the freshly baked bread. Everyone seemed to be of the same mind, and nothing was said until there were five empty bowls stacked on the table.

"That's better." She dabbed her napkin to her lips. "I can think straight again."

"So, what's this letter you've been hiding from us?" Archie asked. "When did it arrive?"

Eliza reached for her handbag to retrieve it. "It's from Mrs Scott's bag."

"Ma's handbag? How? When?" Maggie looked from Eliza to Archie.

"When Henry found it, I had a quick look inside. There was no purse, but I found this." Eliza waved the envelope in the air, but Archie scowled at her.

"Why didn't you keep it with the handbag so we could pass it to the police?"

Eliza rolled her eyes. "What would they do with it? They still think it was an accident."

"Only because we've not told them what we've found. I need to go over there this afternoon."

"Well, you can mention this to them, if it's relevant." Eliza studied the envelope. "It's addressed to Mrs Scott and was sent from Edinburgh."

"Is there a date on it?"

"The fourteenth of August, so last Thursday. A week before she came to St Giles."

"What does it say?" Maggie was on the edge of her seat as Eliza took out the letter and skimmed the contents.

"It's from a solicitor confirming her instruction to sell the property in Cupar."

"She was selling the croft?" Confusion flashed across Maggie's eyes.

"That's what it sounds like ... unless she had more than one."

Maggie shook her head. "No, she didn't. Why would she do that without telling us?"

"Are you sure she hadn't mentioned it to Mr Scott?" Eliza asked.

"I'd be surprised if he knew." Maggie's cheeks coloured. "I must confess I complained every time he got a letter summoning him to Cupar. If he knew she was moving, he'd have told me, to keep me quiet if nothing else."

Archie studied Maggie. "When did Mrs Scott tell you she was visiting?"

"Only at the end of last week."

"So, after she'd received this letter."

Maggie nodded. "Do you think this is why she came?"

"Perhaps the plan was for her to move in with you, but she wanted to wait until she arrived before she said anything." Connie's face was a picture of innocence, but Maggie's eyes grew wide.

"She wouldn't dare. Robert would never have allowed it."

Eliza's brow creased. "Would he have had any choice if Mrs Scott insisted?"

Maggie stood up and walked to the window. "That may explain why she wanted the girls to go home with her, so they could pack up her belongings."

"We don't know that for sure." Archie studied his sister. "We need to talk to Robert first to make sure we're not jumping to the wrong conclusions."

"Yes, you're right." Maggie ran a hand over her head. "Is there any more tea in that pot? I think I need some."

Much to Eliza's relief, the breeze was cool as they made their way back to the headland.

"It's warm work walking up that hill."

"You'll be in good shape by the time we go home."

Eliza bashed Archie on the arm. "You mean I'm not already?"

"All right, even better shape then. Will that do?" He chuckled as Eliza scowled at him. "You didn't need to come, you could have gone directly to the beach and met us down there. We've no idea what these steps will be like."

"So if you found any clues near the top, I'd have to walk up the stairs. No, thank you. Anyway, we're here now. Shall we see if there's anything here?"

With Henry in the lead, the five of them ambled along the headland towards the top of the steps. Eliza stopped when they reached the place they'd seen the disturbed sand.

"Would you say someone's been here since we last looked at this?"

Archie studied the area. "It's certainly changed from earlier, probably someone walking across it to get to the beach."

"It could be someone deliberately trying to hide the marks."

Archie rolled his eyes. "Why do you suspect everything?"

"Somebody has to!"

Henry bent down to examine the footprints. "I don't think it's anything suspicious."

Eliza puffed out her cheeks. "All right, we'll leave it for now. Let's keep going."

Henry led the way. "Take care on the steps. The first dozen or so are quite steep, but after that they flatten out. You can hold on to the rocks near the top to steady yourselves."

"Well, don't rush on ahead. We need to go slowly with these skirts wrapping around our legs."

The steps weren't as treacherous as Eliza expected and less than ten minutes later, Archie was the last of the group to reach the beach.

"Did anyone see anything?"

"Not a thing." Eliza stood with her hands on her hips, staring back at the steps. "After all that effort, too."

"It's not wasted, though," Archie said. "At least we can say there's nothing there."

"That's true. We just need to scour the rocks next."

"What about asking those people?" Connie pointed to several men who were making their way towards them across the beach. "If they were here at the same time yesterday, they may have seen something."

"Connie, you're a marvel." Eliza flashed a smile at her friend. "Will you come with me while the others carry on looking?"

Archie reached for her arm. "You're not approaching strange men on your own. I'll come with you ... and let me do the talking."

"Good afternoon, gentlemen." Archie raised his hat as he approached two of the men. "Can I ask if you were on the beach at around this time yesterday?"

"Aye. I'm down 'ere most afternoons." He turned to his companion. "We both are. Come looking for shells and the like when the tide goes out."

"Did you notice anything unusual yesterday? Any strangers or confrontations, that sort of thing?"

The first man shook his head. "Can't say I did."

"Nor me," his friend said. "It was quiet to be honest, more so than usual with half the village being away."

A third man had joined them but remained silent as a frown settled on his face.

"Did you see something, sir?"

"I cannae be sure." He leaned over to pat the dog standing beside him. "I had him with me as always and found a stick for him. I was stood about here..." he strode over to a place close to the seaweed line "...and threw it towards the rocks. As I watched it drop, I thought there was someone on the path above; not that there's anything unusual in that, but it was only for a second, so I decided I must have imagined it."

"That's interesting, thank you," Archie said.

"Could you tell us what time that was?" Eliza ignored Archie's stare.

"Now you're asking. I was late yesterday and didnae get

here until close on half past two. I probably stayed for an hour or so."

"And the time you thought you saw someone?"

The man paused. "It wasn't long after I got here, so nearer half past two than three o'clock."

Archie put his hand up to stop Eliza. "When you saw them, could you tell whether it was a man or woman?"

"I couldnae be sure, but I would say a man. Besides, what woman would be walking up there on her own?"

"So, there was only one person?"

The man shrugged. "I assumed so, but I couldnae be certain."

"Not to worry, that's very helpful, anyway."

Archie began to move away, but Eliza stopped him.

"One final thing, while you were here, was there anything unusual around the rocks?"

"Unusual? No, I cannae say there was. What are you looking for?"

"Oh, just a man behaving suspiciously."

"No, definitely didn't see anyone like that."

"Or anything lying around that you wouldn't expect?"

The three of them shook their heads.

"Not to worry. Thank you anyway." Eliza watched as the men went on their way. "What do we make of that then?"

"Not a lot." Archie beckoned over Henry and Maggie.

"It does raise some questions, though."

"What did they say?" Henry asked when he joined them.

Eliza took out her paper and pencil and spoke while she wrote her notes. "The man with the dog was here until about half past three, but there was no body on the beach when he left."

Maggie's eyes narrowed. "But Ma had disappeared when I got back to the bench at about half past two."

"Precisely. So, what happened to her between leaving the bench and ending up on the beach sometime after half past three?"

"What about the houses on the headland?" Connie pointed to the few that could be seen. "Maybe someone living there saw her."

Eliza folded up her paper and looked to the top of the cliff. "Or perhaps she'd planned to meet whoever lives there. Called in for a cup of tea, even. Do you know the people who live there, Maggie? And more to the point, would Mrs Scott have known them?"

"Well, yes, I do, but I'm not sure Ma would. Robert may know."

Eliza started to walk away. "We need to speak to them."

"Eliza, stop." Archie stepped forward and took hold of the top of her arms. "This is not your investigation. We have to tell the police and get them to do the questioning. I want you to come back to the inn with me before I get the carriage to St Andrews. In fact, you can come with me. I'm not leaving you here unsupervised."

"The police won't do anything."

"Not if we don't tell them, they won't. Now, come along, I'm not taking no for an answer."

Eliza's cheeks were burning, but there was no point arguing when Archie was in one of these moods, especially not in front of other people. "Very well, I'll tell the police what we know." Eliza turned back towards the road but nearly jumped out of her skin.

"What will you tell us?"

"Sergeant Mitchell, Constable McIntyre, we weren't expecting you back." Archie glanced at Eliza. "We were just coming to see you."

"Don't you worry yourself, Dr Thomson. You said you'd bring the death certificate for the lady you found this morning, but we needed to come back so thought we'd save you the journey."

"I'm sorry for the delay, Sergeant, but it's not ready yet. There's been some debate about the cause of death. Has the post-mortem been completed?"

The sergeant's face twisted. "It's scheduled for tomorrow. What's the problem?"

Eliza put on her most officious voice. "We have reason to believe Mrs Scott's death wasn't an accident."

The sergeant stared at her before turning back to Archie.

"Is that true, sir?"

"I'm afraid it is. After you'd gone, we noticed some bruising around the victim's neck and my wife pointed out that if the body had fallen, it would have been much closer to the rocks than where we found it."

"I'm sure it was just the tide that moved it." The sergeant gave Eliza a patronising smile. "Nothing for you to worry about."

"You mean the tide that travelled further up the beach than that line of seaweed?" Eliza returned the smile, causing the sergeant to stiffen.

"Perhaps someone pulled it away from the water."

"No, they didn't." Maggie stepped forward from behind Archie. "As you know, we found her this morning and the clothes she was wearing were dry. She hadn't been in the sea, and as far as I'm concerned, while the body was on the beach, my brother was the only person to touch it."

Sergeant Mitchell stepped away from the group to study the area. "So, what do you reckon happened?"

Maggie recounted the events of the previous afternoon until she returned to the bench to find Mrs Scott missing.

"The question we were asking when you arrived was, what happened to Mrs Scott once she left the bench? There was a man here earlier with his dog, who said he stayed until about half past three yesterday afternoon, but he saw nothing unusual. If Mrs Scott had disappeared by half past two, what happened to her between then and being found here this morning?"

The constable, who had so far remained silent, stared at Maggie. "So, you were the last one to see her alive? Do you have any witnesses to prove Mrs Scott had gone by the time you went back for her?"

"No, I'm afraid I don't. It was quiet on the top yesterday."

"She has a witness to say she was in the shop, though." Connie stepped closer to Maggie.

"But that doesn't cover the period after she got back to the headland."

"I met my husband on the walk home; that was about half past three. I couldn't have been here throwing the body onto the beach if I was with him."

"And we met them." Connie nodded as if agreeing with herself.

"That doesn't mean you couldn't have killed her and come back later to push her from the cliff."

"Me?" Maggie put a hand to her chest.

Eliza groaned. "Sergeant, forgive me, but did you notice

how far the body was from the base of the headland. It took someone with considerable strength to throw it as far as they did."

"And why would I want her dead?" Maggie's voice squeaked as she spoke.

Sergeant Mitchell turned to study her. "We're not strangers around here, Mrs Scott. We know you had issues with your mother-in-law and to be frank, I'd say Constable McIntyre's hit the nail on the head."

"But that's nonsense. Who told you that?"

The sergeant tapped the side of his nose. "People talk ... and lucky for us they do."

"But there was a strange man hanging around outside the church..."

The same supercilious smile returned to the sergeant's lips. "A stranger. How convenient. Can you give us a description?"

"Well, no. I haven't seen him myself ... but Mrs Baker has."

The sergeant shook his head. "We'll be sure to pay her a visit then ... and her husband. I suggest you don't go disappearing on us; we'll treat any attempt to flee with the utmost suspicion." He raised his cap to Archie. "Good day, sir. We'd appreciate it if you'd call at the station tomorrow so we can sort out the paperwork."

"Of course, Officer. I'll be there."

"So much for involving the police." Eliza watched the officers walk away as she spoke to Archie. "When will you learn?"

Maggie grabbed her brother's hands. "They can't accuse me. I wouldn't kill her. I wouldn't kill anyone."

"I know you wouldn't." Archie put an arm around his sister's shoulders. "They won't accuse you, they were just checking you had an alibi."

"But I don't."

Eliza narrowed her eyes. "Don't worry, you've got me and Connie on the case. We won't let you down."

"And me," Henry added.

Eliza nodded. "Exactly. The real killer won't get away with it."

Archie's face was stern. "Eliza, I told you to leave it."

"And have them arrest your sister? Not if there's anything we can do to help. You said yourself, you don't get murders around here; they've probably never investigated one before."

"We don't know that."

Eliza moved her hand to link it through Archie's arm. "I'd say we can be fairly sure, but relax, they won't even realise we're helping them."

CHAPTER NINE

B y the time they'd walked Maggie home and arrived back at the inn, the church bells were ringing for four o'clock.

"Gracious, we'd better get a move on." Eliza hurried to their usual table in the empty bar. "We've only got an hour before we're due at your parents' house and I for one could do with a cup of tea."

"Ooh yes, me too," Connie said.

"What's tonight in aid of, anyway?" Eliza asked as she sat down. "We saw everyone last night. Are we going to be spending every evening with them?"

"I doubt it," Archie said as he joined them. "It was Fraser who invited us round; Ma wasn't terribly keen on the idea."

"More like she doesn't want me there. I'm sure she'd be delighted if you and Henry turned up on your own."

"Must I go?" Henry's shoulders slumped. "I've arranged to see the others tonight."

"If I'm going, you are too, for a little while at least," Eliza said. "I imagine Rabbie and Callum will be there, anyway, even if they didn't know about it last night."

Henry tutted. "I suppose so, although it's rather insensitive having a gathering under the circumstances. I doubt we'll see Aunty Maggie and Mr Scott."

Eliza grimaced. "He has a point."

"Maybe he does, but you're not getting out of it that easily. Even if we don't stay, we need to see how everyone is."

Eliza paused while a tea tray was put down in front of them. "Very well, but if we must go, perhaps we can use the time to find out about the neighbours."

"No, we can't." Archie's voice was stern. "Eliza, this is my family, not a game."

"Exactly, and the police think your sister might be a killer. I'm sure everyone will want to help, even if you don't."

Archie sighed. "You know I do, but I want it done properly."

Eliza picked up the teapot and began to pour. "In that case it's a good job Connie and I are happy to help."

As the bell struck the final chime for five o'clock. Archie held open the front door of the inn and ushered the family outside.

"That's one good thing about living here," Eliza said as she passed him. "You never have far to walk. We'll be there before anyone realises we're late."

"Do you think they'll have heard about Mrs Scott?" Connie asked.

Eliza's mouth dropped open as she stared at Archie. "Gosh, I hadn't even considered that."

"No, neither had I." Archie ran a hand over his face. "I should have called to tell them. I don't suppose there's much we can do about it now; we'll just have to give them the details when we get there ... and please be delicate if you ask questions. They'll all be in shock."

Archie pushed open his parents' front door and as soon as he walked into the living room, Jean hurried over and put her arms around him.

"Archie, you're here. Maggie's told us what happened, and that you had to examine the body. It must have been awful."

"I can't say it was pleasant, but it's all part of the job."

"Have you seen Maggie?" Eliza asked.

"Yes, she's here." Jean glanced around the room. "Somewhere. She called as I was about to leave home and told me about the *accident*."

"She's here?" Archie said. "I must admit, I didn't expect that. How is she?"

Jean shook her head. "Very tearful. She originally said she wouldn't be here because Mr Scott was too upset to join us. But then she turned up about ten minutes ago muttering something about the police thinking she was the murderer."

Eliza nodded. "That's what they suggested. It's obviously ludicrous, but it looks like we'll need to prove she isn't."

Jean gasped. "How will we do that?"

Archie rolled his eyes at his sister. "We have told the police, but Eliza's well practised in these things, aren't you, my dear?"

"Really?" Jean's eyes widened. "You've never told me that."

Eliza's cheeks flushed. "No, it's not the sort of thing you put in a letter."

"And she has two willing helpers. Mrs Appleton and..." Archie glanced over his shoulder. "Where's Henry gone?"

76

"All his cousins are here," Jean said. "I imagine they've dragged him off to the kitchen to get away from us old fogeys."

Eliza laughed. "I'm sure he'll be delighted."

Jean released Archie and took hold of Eliza's arm. "Come and sit down and tell us what you want us to do."

Eliza and Connie accepted two chairs that had been positioned between Jean and Mrs Thomson.

"Are these new? I don't remember them being here the other night." Eliza ran her hand across the striped fabric of the chair.

"They're mine," Jean said. "We brought them over earlier. Now, I've a pot of tea brewing, let me go and pour it before we start."

"Start what?" Mrs Thomson suddenly sat up straight.

"We want to talk about Mrs Scott's death, Ma, and the fact the police think our Maggie had something to do with it."

"I'll just go and tell them they're wrong. She wouldn't do anything like that." Mrs Thomson dabbed her eyes with a handkerchief. "Not that they should need telling; they should know better."

"We all agree with that, but Eliza may help make it more official."

"Humph. What does she know about the ways around here? She hasn't got a clue."

Eliza squirmed in her seat as Mrs Thomson purposely looked past her.

"It's got to be worth a try, Ma." Fraser arrived by the fireplace with three glasses of Scotch balanced between his hands. He offered one to Archie before passing the other to his pa. "Here you go, this is on me. I'm sick of waiting for the old skinflint to get his bottle out."

77

"Less of your cheek." There was no amusement on Mr Thomson's face. "It's about time you gave me a drink instead of expecting mine every time you visit."

"I'm sure you're both very generous." Archie raised his glass. "Good health."

"Slainte!" Fraser clinked his glass against Archie's. "Have you forgotten your mother tongue! Now then, tell us what's been going on."

"I've told you." Maggie bustled into the room and squeezed onto an overly wide chair in the corner of the room, which was already occupied by Jean.

Fraser rolled his eyes. "I want to hear the non-hysterical version if you don't mind."

"Don't be like that," Archie said. "On this occasion the hysterics are probably justified."

"They are, but thankfully Mrs Appleton's been standing up for me." Maggie smiled at Connie. "She defended me when the police were trying to accuse me of being the killer."

"I'm sure that's very kind of you, Mrs Appleton, but how do you know it wasn't my sister?"

"Fraser!" Mrs Thomson's voice boomed across the room. "How can you even joke about something like that?"

"It wasn't a joke, Ma. Mrs Appleton hardly knows our Maggie, so how can she vouch for her?"

"Well..." Connie's cheeks were red "...because she doesn't seem the type. And if the only reason the police can find for her to kill Mrs Scott is because she didn't like Mr Scott visiting Cupar so often, it's not good enough. Eliza always says you need a strong motive."

Eliza nodded. "You're absolutely right, Connie."

Fraser looked to Archie, who was standing beside him. "But who on earth would want Mrs Scott dead?"

"That's the question, isn't it?" Eliza didn't miss the look on Fraser's face as he turned to her, but she ignored it. "If we're to prove it wasn't Maggie, we need to work out who else had a motive ... and the opportunity."

"But why do the police think Maggie would want her dead?" Mrs Thomson finally looked at Eliza. "What did you say to them?"

Eliza counted to three. "I didn't say anything. We only told them that it didn't look like an accident. Someone else must have said something because it was them who told us Maggie wasn't fond of Mrs Scott, not the other way around. Otherwise, if they're based in St Andrews, how would they know?"

Mr Stewart coughed. "Perhaps I can answer that. Robert was in The Coach House the other day saying how he'd been summoned to pick up his ma from Cupar and he commented that Maggie was furious about it."

"He said that?" Maggie sat bolt upright. "How dare he go around gossiping about me. He wasn't best pleased himself. Did he mention that?"

"I-I don't remember."

"Which means he didn't. Wait 'til I get home. I can already tell he agrees with the police. He thinks that if I hadn't left her alone on the bench, she'd still be alive."

"That doesn't sound like Robert," Mrs Thomson said. "He's usually very considerate."

"Except when it comes to his mother." Maggie spat out her words.

"Forgive me for asking, but would Mr Scott have any

reason for wanting his ma dead?" Eliza paused as everyone stared at her. "Well? If I'm not mistaken, the silence suggests that it may not be as strange a question as I thought."

Maggie finally spoke. "I probably shouldn't be saying this, but his ma did know how to upset him."

"But surely he wouldn't kill her?" Archie raised an eyebrow at his sister, but she shrugged.

"If he thinks *I* killed her, even though I'm not capable of anything like that, then I've no reason to defend him. He disliked her as much as I did."

"All right, let's not worry about that now; we can speak to him later." Eliza pulled a pencil and paper from her bag. "What can any of you tell me about the people who live in the houses on the headland? Those overlooking the sea."

"Mr Stewart's your man for that. Isn't that right, son?" Mr Thomson smacked his lips as he finished his Scotch.

"I suppose so."

"What about the particularly big house that has pride of place on the top?"

"Clifftop House," Maggie informed her.

"That sounds very grand. Who lives there?"

Mr Stewart rolled backwards and forwards on the balls of his feet. "That's Mr Watson, a nice man."

"Can you tell me anything about him?"

Mr Stewart shrugged. "There's not much to tell. He's our landlord; decent enough sort."

"When it suits him." Maggie turned to Eliza. "By all accounts, he's pleasant when he's in company but if you meet him on his own, he's a miserable devil. Like someone else I know…"

"He's not that bad." Mr Stewart scowled at Maggie. "And that's enough about Robert. He's been through a lot lately."

Eliza exchanged glances with Archie as Maggie slumped back in her chair.

"All right, let's start again." Archie stepped into the middle of the group. "Mr Stewart, you said Mr Watson's your landlord."

"Yes, that's right."

"Is he a member of the landed gentry?" Connie's cheeks flushed as she spoke.

"Oh no, nothing like that. He's as normal as the rest of us. Used to play the church organ, actually, and happens to be a good businessman."

Connie sighed. "Thank goodness for that."

"Quite." Eliza gave Connie a sideways glance. "We had more than enough of them last year."

"I don't know why he needs such a big house, though," Mr Thomson said. "He's at The Coach House every lunchtime and evening. He's never at home."

"His wife can't be pleased," Connie said.

"Unfortunately, Mrs Watson's no longer with us." Mr Stewart's voice softened. "She passed away a few years ago; that's why he spends all his time at The Coach House."

Archie gave Eliza a pointed glance. "Which means that if we want to speak with him, I'll do it. I'm not having you going into a bar talking to strange men, certainly not unchaperoned."

"I should think not." Mrs Thomson's face curled up in disgust. "Chaperoned or not."

Eliza bit down on her lip and counted to three. "We'll talk

about that later. What about his next-door neighbour? Do you know him, too?"

"Mr Burns. Another one who's usually at The Coach House with us."

Eliza studied Mr Stewart. "Do you drink with them as well?"

"I'm not in there as often as they are."

"You don't do too badly," Jean said. "I hardly see you."

"Were you in there with them yesterday?" Eliza held her pencil poised over her paper.

"Aye. It was a typical day. Fishing and gutting in the morning, in the bar over lunch and then back to mend the nets for the rest of the afternoon."

"And were you all there together?"

Mr Stewart nodded. "All of us who live down here. You saw us on the beach when you called before the party."

"Yes, of course." Eliza's forehead furrowed. "Does Mr Scott usually join you?"

"Aye, sometimes, when he's not working or up in Cupar ... or our Maggie hasn't got him doing something."

"I haven't had him doing any chores for months so don't look at me like that."

"Leave her alone." Jean patted her sister's hand. "You've enough drinking pals without worrying about Robert."

Eliza spoke before Mr Stewart could respond. "So, who else is usually with you?"

"It's a fisherman's resting place." Mr Thomson tapped his empty glass on the arm of his chair. "They're all in there most nights."

"You mean the men from the other cottages on the beach?"

"That's them."

"And do you join them, Mr Thomson?"

"What if I do?"

Eliza's face flushed. "No reason, but if we're looking for evidence that Maggie had nothing to do with Mrs Scott's death, I need to understand who knows who, and who I should talk to."

"Well, I saw nothing so don't come talking to me."

"No, right, I'll make a note of that."

While she was writing, Connie leaned across to her. "If the fishermen were working on their nets, they may have seen something. You can see the headland and houses from where they work."

Mr Stewart's stance stiffened. "We've no time for gawping. When we're with the boats, we have our heads down, gutting fish or mending the nets."

Eliza regained her composure. "That's as maybe, but someone could have seen something, even if they didn't realise it was important." She looked across to Archie. "We'd better speak to the fishermen, as well."

"Don't forget the minister," Jean said. "Not that I'm suggesting he's the murderer, but the church and manse are on the headland so he may have spotted something."

Eliza's forehead furrowed. "Manse?"

Jean chuckled. "You English! The minister's house."

"Ah, right. And what's the minister's name?"

"Reverend Rennie."

Mr Stewart shot Jean a venomous glance. "I'm sure he won't want to be troubled. He's getting on a bit now; his memory's not what it was."

"Of course it is." Mrs Thomson roused herself from the

snooze she'd fallen into. "His mind's as sharp as anyone else's. Just because he's old, doesn't mean he's senile."

"Well, we'll go and see him, we need to speak to Mr Baker, anyway."

Connie whispered behind her hand. "What about the stranger?"

"Ah, yes, thank you, I was about to ask about him. Mrs Baker in the shop said she's seen a stranger loitering outside the church for the last couple of days. Have any of you seen him?"

As one, everyone in the room shook their heads.

"I only go up there on a Sunday, so don't ask me," Mrs Thomson said.

"Do you have a description of him?" Jean asked.

"Not really, other than he's a man of average height with greying hair."

Jean laughed. "That could be anyone in the village. The minister may know something about him, though. The church has a habit of attracting undesirables."

"That's a good point." Eliza made a final note on her paper before folding it up and putting it in her bag. "Well, unless you have anything else to add, I'd say that will keep us busy tomorrow." She turned to Maggie. "I'll call in and speak to Mr Scott then as well. It wouldn't surprise me if he knows more than he's letting on."

CHAPTER TEN

Archie and Henry had finished breakfast by the time Eliza and Connie arrived downstairs.

"What on earth have you been doing? I'd almost given up on you."

"I'm sorry, Dr Thomson, it was my fault." Connie straightened her skirt as she sat down. "I misplaced my necklace and Eliza kindly waited for me."

"Well, I hope you found it."

Connie touched the pendant hanging from the chain around her neck. "Yes, I did thank you."

Archie pushed his chair away from the table. "I hate to leave you, but I must be going. I promised the police I'd call with the papers for the death. I hope I won't be long, but even if they don't rush, I should be back for midday. Shall I meet you here?"

Eliza's shoulders slumped. "I'd forgotten you had to go over there. I wanted to speak to witnesses this morning."

"Depending on who they are, you still can. Why don't you start with Maggie and Mr Scott? And take Henry with you."

Connie pulled a face. "I do hope he and Mrs Scott aren't still blaming each other."

"I'm sure Maggie can stand up for herself; see you later." Archie picked up his hat and with a nod of the head left them.

"You're very quiet." Eliza glanced at Henry as she spread butter on a piece of toast. "What are you doing this morning?"

"Coming with you. What else do you think I'm doing?"

Eliza shrugged. "After last night, I wondered if you were meeting up with your cousins again. They seem keen to spend time with you."

"They're a nice crowd, but I only agreed to meet them after luncheon. I figured we'd be done by then."

"Did you now? It depends what we find out this morning. We go home next week so we can't sit around every afternoon; I'd like this all sorted out."

Henry stood up. "You'd better hurry up then. I'll wait for you outside."

Maggie's front door was open when they arrived, but Eliza still knocked before they let themselves in.

"Is there anyone home?"

Maggie bustled into the kitchen, her hair in disarray. "Oh, it's you, come in and sit down; I'm in the back pegging out some washing."

"Take your time." Eliza waited for Henry to pull out a chair for her. "Is Mr Scott in? It's him we're here to see."

Maggie's lips set in a hard line. "He was, but he went out. I've no idea where to, but that was about an hour ago."

Eliza's smile slipped. "Never mind, we'll wait. You finish your washing."

"I wonder where he's gone," Connie said once Maggie disappeared.

"Who knows?" Eliza pursed her lips. "He seems a strange chap."

"You can't be too harsh on him; he has just lost his mother." Henry wandered to the window and gazed out. "There he is. I'd say he's been for a walk on the beach. He probably just needed some air."

"Is he coming here?"

Henry returned to his seat. "It looks like it."

A moment later, they heard footsteps in the hallway and Mr Scott walked into the kitchen.

"Mr Scott." Eliza managed her most endearing smile. "Forgive us for intruding but we were hoping to have a word with you ... if you don't mind."

"Why should I mind?"

"Well, with what's happened, I expect you're still upset."

Mr Scott joined them at the table. "Not any more. I've done a lot of thinking since yesterday and realise it was no more than she deserved. She enjoyed making people's lives a misery. Mine included. If she was murdered, it probably serves her right."

Eliza stared at Mr Scott, her mouth open before she quickly closed it. "I'm sure none of us deserve to die however much we upset people."

Mr Scott shrugged. "Whether she did or not, it's a moot point now. Someone clearly wanted her dead."

"Well ... yes. I suppose so. Have you any idea who that might be?"

Mr Scott shook his head. "None, but now I've got over the shock, I'd like to shake his hand."

Eliza raised her eyebrows. "You think it was a man?"

"I assume it was; women don't go around throwing each other off cliffs, do they?"

"Not usually, but we can't completely rule it out. We know the time of death was after two o'clock on Thursday afternoon and before ten in the evening. What were you doing between those hours?"

He stared into the distance. "I came home with Ma at about half past one and had a cup of tea. You were here, I seem to remember."

Eliza nodded.

"After that, I sat by the fire until turned three and then I walked to the shop to send a telegram."

"A telegram?"

"I should have been in work, but because of Ma I had to miss a day. I always pick the coal up from a store in St Andrews and needed to send apologies to the boss."

"So it was when you came out of the shop that you bumped into Maggie?"

A vacant expression crossed Mr Scott's face as he stared at Eliza.

"We met you in the street if you remember."

"Yes, of course, I'm sorry. Everything feels a bit of a blur at the moment."

Eliza nodded. "I'm sure it does."

"Did you see anything unusual while you were walking to the shop?" Henry asked. "Anyone you didn't know, perhaps."

"No, I can't say I did. It was unusually quiet actually."

"Have you spoken to Maggie since yesterday?" Eliza asked.

"I've hardly seen him." Maggie walked into the kitchen,

fixing her hair as she did. "Whenever I do, he blames me for Ma's death."

Mr Scott stood up and banged his hand on the table. "You were the one who left her on her own near the drop..." He took a deep breath and sat down again. "But the way she died, I realise it couldn't have been you."

Maggie bustled over to the sink. "Thank goodness for that."

Eliza watched as she filled the kettle. "Have you mentioned the letter to him?"

"Letter? What letter?" Mr Scott's eyes flicked between Maggie and Eliza.

"No, not yet. We were out last night and I went straight to bed when I came in."

"What letter?"

Eliza opened her handbag and placed the letter in front of him. "We found this in Mrs Scott's handbag. It's from a solicitor in Edinburgh saying he's begun the process of selling her house in Cupar."

Incomprehension settled on Mr Scott's face. "She was selling the croft? Why would she do that?"

"Possibly because she planned on moving back here?"

"She was selling everything and hadn't told me?" Mr Scott's brow creased as he read the letter. "After everything I did. She said I had to make it weatherproof for the winter."

"Maybe she did, although perhaps it wasn't for her benefit."

"Isn't that typical?" Maggie planted a hand on her hip. "You kept going over there and doing whatever she wanted and yet this is how she treated you."

"How was I to know?"

"I told you she was up to something."

"You've been telling me that for twenty-five years..."

Eliza held up her hands. "Please, this isn't helping. I think it's safe to assume neither of you knew Mrs Scott's plans, but we need to find the motive behind her death. Someone must have wanted her out of the way. Could anyone have known she was moving back?"

Mr Scott and Maggie stared at each other.

"She didn't keep in touch with anyone here, as far as I know," Mr Scott said.

Eliza nodded. "It was only a thought. If you think of anything else, will you let me know?"

"Won't you stay for a cup of tea?" Maggie took the kettle off the range.

"We'd better not. We want to visit Mr Baker and Reverend Rennie before midday. It looks like things might be trickier than we imagined."

Eliza and Connie paused for breath as they reached the top of the hill.

"It's not that steep," Henry called to them.

"Not if you're a young man. Wait until you're our age."

Henry laughed. "All right then, two minutes. Where do you want to go first?"

"Given that we're stood outside the *manse*, why don't we go there ... or should we try the church? I wonder where the reverend's most likely to be."

Henry ran the twenty yards to the church before he turned back. "The door's open, we could try in there."

With their breath restored, the three of them walked in single file up the church path to a heavy wooden door. Henry opened it further and ushered them inside.

"I don't suppose there's anyone here. The only candles lit are on the altar." Eliza blinked several times to adjust her eyes to the gloom.

Henry walked down the right-hand aisle and peered into a number of crevices before he beckoned them forward. "There's an office here." He pushed the door open and popped his head inside. "Nobody's here, though."

Eliza's heart raced as the darkness closed in around her. "I suggest we go then. The reverend must be next door."

"Don't you want to look...?"

"No, thank you. We're obviously the only ones here."

With a final glance around, Henry nodded and escorted them back to the church door. Once outside, Eliza breathed a sigh of relief.

"That's better."

"You weren't scared, were you?" Henry winked at Connie.

"Of course not."

"You're just happier to be outside, aren't you?" Connie linked her arm through Eliza's.

"Yes, I am, thank you ... and less of your cheek!" She flicked a hand at Henry. "Now, lead the way to the manse."

The gate to the back garden was open, and Henry disappeared through it before he returned and called Eliza and Connie to join him.

"He's in the garden."

The minister looked up as they approached, keeping hold of the dead rose he was about to clip from the bush in front of him.

"Good morning, Reverend. I hope you don't mind us disturbing you."

With a swift click of the scissors, the elderly clergyman turned around to give them his full attention. "Not at all. What may I do for you?"

Eliza made the introductions, making sure to mention that she and Henry were related, by marriage at least, to the late Mrs Scott.

"Ah yes. What a terrible accident. Her son called this morning to arrange the funeral."

"He did?" Eliza's eyes flicked to Henry. "He didn't mention it."

"Did he give you any details of what happened?" Henry asked.

The minister stepped forward to the next rose bush. "He said that not long after she'd arrived in the village she'd walked up to the headland and then slipped and fallen to the beach."

"So, he didn't tell you the police were involved?"

"The police? Good gracious, no."

Eliza raised an eyebrow. "Ah, well, I'm sorry to be the bearer of bad news, but we don't believe Mrs Scott's death was an accident. All the evidence suggests she was murdered."

"Murdered?" The minister took a step backwards, causing Connie to catch hold of him before he fell.

"Oh my. Are you all right? Let's get you to a seat." Connie nodded towards a bench alongside the back wall of the house.

The minister's hands trembled as they led him to the seat. "Surely there must be some mistake?"

Eliza shook her head. "I'm afraid not. That's why we're here. Unfortunately, the police are rather busy at the moment and so with Mrs Scott being part of the family we offered to talk to people to see if they'd seen anything or anyone out of the ordinary."

"Gracious, what a terrible business." The minister's hands continued to tremble as he rested them on his knees.

"Did you see anything unusual on the headland or around the church yesterday afternoon or evening?" Eliza asked.

"Yesterday?" The minister screwed up his already wrinkled forehead. "No, I won't have done. I was in the garden most of the day and when I went indoors, I was in the kitchen, which overlooks the back."

"And nobody came to the house?"

"Not that I know of. Why?"

"We've heard a report of a stranger loitering outside the church. Might you have seen anyone looking suspicious?"

The minister seemed very frail as he shook his head. "No, no one."

"Did you go to the church yesterday?" Henry asked.

"Well, yes, I was there in the morning to open up and light a few candles, but that was it."

"Didn't you lock up again?"

The minister clucked his tongue. "Yes, of course I did, but I didn't see any strangers."

Eliza stood up. "Thank you, Reverend. We'll leave you in peace. Actually, before we do, might we speak with your housekeeper?"

Again, the old man shook his head. "With it being summer, many of the parishioners are away for the week and so I let her take a few days off. She has family in St Andrews, you see."

"So, you're looking after yourself?" Henry's eyes were wide.

"She left the pantry well stocked and she's back on Monday. She told me not to worry about the cleaning." He chuckled to himself. "For once I did as she said."

The church bells were ringing for eleven o'clock as they walked out to the road; Henry held open the gate for them.

"He looks as if he should have hung up his cassock years ago."

Eliza couldn't argue. "I suppose it's quiet enough up here for him."

"Apart from the occasional murder."

Eliza puffed out her cheeks. "He did look rather shocked. I hope he's all right."

"Oh, so do I. He looked such a dear old man." Connie smiled to herself. "It's as well he didn't see anything; it could have killed him."

Henry's mouth twisted. "Crikey, that's not a very cheerful thing to say."

"But she has a point," Eliza said. "I'd say it's a good job he keeps himself to himself."

"So, shall we go to the shop now?" Henry asked. "This Mrs Baker is such a gossip, let's hope she has more information for us."

Eliza laughed. "I'm sure she'd be delighted to talk about the matter for hours, but it's Mr Baker we want to speak to."

Henry tutted as he pushed on the shop door and held it open for Eliza and Connie. A man standing behind a counter to the right looked up.

"Good morning, ladies ... and sir. What can I do for you?"

Eliza put on her best smile. "Actually, we've come to talk to you. I presume you're Mr Baker."

"I am that, although you have me at a disadvantage."

"Forgive me. I'm Mrs Thomson and this is my son Henry and companion, Mrs Appleton. We're here visiting my husband's family, which has unfortunately coincided with the death of Mrs Scott. Am I right in thinking you've heard about it?"

Mr Baker sucked air through his teeth. "Yes, indeed, it was most shocking."

"You probably know Mrs Scott was part of the Thomson family, her being Maggie's mother-in-law, and so we said we'd ask around to find out if anyone had any information about what happened."

"And prove that young Mrs Scott isn't guilty, I imagine?"

"Ah, you've heard about that." Eliza glanced at Connie. "Yes, unfortunately, Maggie was the last person to see her mother-in-law alive and the police have taken it as a sign of her guilt. Naturally, we don't believe that."

"It would seem most peculiar, if you ask me, but you're better off talking to the wife. I was in St Andrews for most of the afternoon yesterday and so I can't tell you anything of relevance."

"We've already spoken to Mrs Baker, but we wondered if you could confirm what time you left the shop and when you got back." Eliza took the notepaper from her handbag.

"Now, let me think. I went out straight after lunch, which would have been about half past one and arrived home at about four."

"So you were driving towards St Andrews between half past one and two o'clock? Was anyone travelling in the opposite direction?"

"Into St Giles, you mean? Well, there were other carriages on the road, but I didn't pay much attention to them. It's not uncommon to have visitors coming to the village."

"Was anybody walking?"

Mr Baker screwed up his face. "No, I don't think so."

"Can I ask what you did once you got back?" Henry asked.

"Now then, first of all, I tended the horses, gave them a brushing down and some fodder, and then put the carriage away. By then it was teatime and so we sat down in the kitchen and had a nice bit of boiled ham."

"Did you go out again later?"

He shook his head. "I didn't see daylight after that. I was in the cellar checking on the stock; it was getting dark by the time I came upstairs again."

"Gracious, you must have a lot of stock," Connie said.

Mr Baker tapped his finger on the side of his nose. "Don't tell the missus, but I have a little corner to myself down there." He winked at Henry. "You'll know what I mean."

Eliza rolled her eyes. "At least she knows where you are." She looked down at her notes. "Given you were out all afternoon, I wonder if we could ask Mrs Baker a further question. Is she free?"

Mrs Baker had been making bread in the back room and appeared to have wiped most of the flour down the front of her apron when she'd been called.

"We're sorry to disturb you," Eliza said, "but may we ask you another question about Thursday afternoon?"

Mrs Baker smiled. "Oh, of course you can, dearie. The bread's rising now, so we've plenty of time. What would you like to know?"

"Did Mr Scott come in asking you to send a telegram?"

"A telegram. Gracious, no. Mr Baker usually sees to that and so if I'd done it, I'd remember."

"And he didn't come in once you were back?" Eliza studied Mr Baker.

"No. As I said. I didn't come into the shop."

"That's interesting." Eliza paused before putting away her pencil and paper. "This is the only place in the village to send a telegram, I presume."

"Aye. It's either here or in St Andrews."

Eliza fastened her handbag. "Thank you. That's very helpful."

CHAPTER ELEVEN

Eliza raised her eyebrows at Connie and Henry as they left the shop and headed back down the hill.

"Well ... what did you make of that?"

"What's he hiding?" Connie said.

Henry shrugged. "I thought it was strange when he told us he'd sat at home for an hour before going out to send the telegram."

"Exactly." Eliza's brow furrowed as she walked. "For one thing, why didn't he walk to the shop with them?"

"Or get Aunty Maggie to do it while she was out."

"Or ... why didn't he just go to work?" Connie glanced at Eliza. "What man sits at home when they've a job they should be doing?"

Eliza nodded. "You both make good points. We'll ask him later, but first I'm hoping Archie's back from St Andrews. We need to eat."

Henry stopped and stared back up the hill. "We were going to visit the houses up there."

Eliza clapped a hand to her head. "Confound it, I was so

busy thinking about the telegram, I forgot." She looked at the steep incline. "There is another option. I just need to speak to your father first; let's go back to The Coach House."

Archie was waiting for them by the reception desk when they arrived.

"Ah, good, you're here. I'm rather hungry." He extended his arm to usher them into the dining room. "Shall we go in?"

"Actually–" Eliza stopped "–could we eat in the bar area?"

Archie stared at her. "You and Mrs Appleton in the bar at this time? I don't think so."

"Please. I wouldn't ask if it wasn't important ... and the landlady said we could."

"It would be nice for a change." Connie's cheeks were pink. "And Eliza wouldn't ask without good reason."

"Thank you, Connie, there is. I'll tell you why when we sit down."

Reluctantly, Archie led them to their usual table in the corner of the room and held out a chair for Eliza. "Now, are you going to tell me what you're up to?"

She sat down and waited for everyone else to take their seats. "We've had quite an interesting morning, but we were so distracted when we came out of the shop that we forgot to call at the houses on the headland. Mr Stewart mentioned that the men who live there are often in here and so I thought that if we were too, we could speak to them."

Archie didn't look convinced. "I don't want you talking to any of them."

"I won't. We'll just sit and listen, see if they have anything interesting to say." She flashed him her best smile. "How did you get on with the police?"

Archie sighed. "All I did was write a statement saying I'd examined the body and when we found it at eight yesterday morning it had been dead for at least twelve hours. They don't have the results of the post-mortem yet and so we couldn't put a cause of death on the certificate."

"Will the coroner do that?"

"Either that, or they can bring the paperwork to me. I'm not driving over there every day on the off chance the post-mortem's been done. I'm here to visit my parents, not run around after them."

"Exactly." Eliza patted his hand. "Why don't you call on them this afternoon?"

Archie's eyes narrowed. "Why? What are you up to?"

"Nothing." Eliza arranged a napkin on her knee.

"It sounds like you're trying to get me out of the way."

She sat back in her seat as a plate of fish and chips was put down in front of her. "Of course I'm not, but you should spend time together before Fraser leaves; and it'd be better all round if I wasn't with you."

Henry picked up his knife and fork. "I've arranged to meet Rabbie and Callum at two o'clock by the boats. We won't know until then if Niall and Ross can join us or if they'll be busy net mending again."

"It's nice that you're getting along so well," Connie said. "What do you do when you're together?"

Henry shrugged. "Not much, really. To be honest, I don't have a lot in common with them. They're nice enough though..."

He was interrupted when a group of men walked into the room and took up what looked like their usual positions at the bar.

"So, what exactly did it say in the paper?" A muscular man with dark grey hair and a weathered face took a seat between the bar and the door.

"That police had found the body of a Mrs Scott washed up on the beach yesterday morning." A man with a face just as weatherworn sat alongside him as the barman put two tankards of ale on the bar. "I'll take a Scotch with that. It's not every day you hear of a dead body around here."

"It wasn't Maggie Scott, was it?"

"No, it said *previously* from St Giles..."

"Have you seen the paper this morning?" Eliza leaned forward to whisper. "I never even thought to check."

Everyone shook their heads as the first man continued talking.

"If it's the one we used to know, what's she doing here? I thought she was never coming back."

A third, smartly dressed man with silver grey hair and a complexion that suggested he didn't make a living from the sea picked up a glass of Scotch. "By the sounds of it, she should have stayed away. She must have forgotten about the drop from the headland. That's what happens when you move to the middle of nowhere."

"I don't suppose Robert or his missus will lose any sleep over it and we may even get our coal on time again." The second man paused as the front door opened and Mr Stewart joined them. "Here you are. Those nets looked like they'd take you all afternoon."

Mr Stewart laughed. "No point having sons if you don't make them earn their keep."

Eliza raised her eyebrows at Henry. "It doesn't look like Niall and Ross will be spending much time with you later."

"I think you're right..."

"Ah, Dr Thomson. I'd forgotten you might be here." Mr Stewart walked over to the table and shook Archie's hand before turning back to his friends. "Everyone, this is my brother-in-law, Dr Thomson, and his family." He pointed to the men at the bar. "Mr McKay, by the wall and then Mr Dowie. They're both from the cottages near me, and this is Mr Watson from Clifftop House." Mr Stewart checked around the room. "Where's Mr Cargill?"

"He's on his way," Mr McKay said. "Said he wanted a word with Mr Burns about something."

Archie stood up to shake everyone by the hand before he introduced Eliza, Connie and Henry. "I'm sorry to disturb your drinking time, but the bar was empty when we sat down."

"No need to apologise," Mr Watson said. "We don't get many visitors around here; it's nice to talk to somebody new when we have the chance."

"You'll have heard about Mrs Scott's death then, I imagine," Mr McKay said. "Can you give us any more details?"

"I've not seen the newspaper and so I don't know what you've read."

Mr Dowie banged his empty glass on the bar. "They didn't say much, they never do. Just that the old dear was found dead. Did she fall from the headland?"

Archie paused and glanced at Eliza as the two men she presumed to be Mr Burns and Mr Cargill joined them. As with the other men, it was clear who was the fisherman of the two.

"What kept you?" Mr Watson jerked his thumb towards Mr Dowie. "He's had his first Scotch already."

Mr Burns was immaculately dressed in a shirt, tie and neatly tailored jacket. "Just a bit of business; I'll tell you about it later." He raised his eyebrows at Mr Watson. "What have we missed?"

"We were talking about Mrs Scott's body being found on the beach. I take it you read this morning's newspaper?"

"I did and it was quite a shock."

Mr Watson extended his hand towards Archie. "This is Dr Thomson, Billy Thomson's lad who disappeared to London. He was about to tell us what he knows."

The men pulled up their bar stools and turned to face him.

"To be honest, we're not certain about the cause of death, but we don't think it was an accident."

"They reckon it was murder!" Mr Stewart gave his companions a knowing look.

"Murder? Why would anyone want her dead?" Mr Dowie indicated to the barman for another Scotch. "In fact, how did anyone know she was here? To my knowledge, no one's seen her around these parts for over twenty years."

"Did you all know her?" Henry asked.

"Och, aye," Mr Cargill said. "We were all youngsters together. Well, all except Mr Stewart." He nudged Mr Watson in the ribs. "In fact, some of us knew her slightly better than the rest. I remember when she used to pop in to church pretending to want a word with the reverend. She only ever did it when you were practising the organ."

Mr Dowie threw back his head with laughter. "I'd

forgotten about that. You were quite a pair back in ... when was it ... around the early fifties?"

Mr Watson shrugged. "Something like that."

"My, she was quite a catch back then. She had her pick of men, but she was totally smitten with you." Mr Burns eyed his friend. "She aged well, too. I'll admit it now, I was jealous of you when you were a couple."

Mr Watson grimaced. "I still had black hair and a spring in my step fifty years ago."

"So did she."

The men roared with laughter until Mr Watson stopped. "I'm sorry, ladies, forgive us for being so crude. We're not used to having the fairer sex in the bar."

Archie stood up. "No, quite. If you'll excuse my wife and her friend, they'd be better in the dining room."

Eliza was sure Archie flinched when she glared at him. "Actually, would you mind if I stayed for a few more minutes? The family are obviously upset about Mrs Scott's death and we'd like to ask if anyone saw anything on Thursday that could help us find the killer."

Archie gave a sigh of resignation and sat down as Mr McKay looked at his fellow fishermen. "As I remember, we had a fairly typical day. We got back to shore at about nine o'clock and stayed on the beach sorting out the fish until we came in here about noon."

Mr Dowie nodded. "Aye, we did, and then we sorted out the nets after we left here."

"And did you notice anyone acting strangely?"

Mr McKay shook his head. "Not me."

"Mr Cargill, what about you?"

There was a brief hesitation. "My eyes aren't as good as

they used to be and so I never see anything out of the ordinary."

Eliza nodded. "What time did you leave the bar?"

Mr Watson shrugged. "We all left sometime between two and half past."

"And would you have gone straight home?"

"I did."

Mr Burns leaned forward in his seat. "And I was with him. We had some business to attend to."

Eliza made a note on her paper before Archie stood up again.

"Are you finished now?"

"Not quite." She put down her pencil. "Mr Burns, you said Mrs Scott had aged well. Had you seen her recently?"

"I did as it happens. In fact, it was on Thursday as we were walking home." He indicated to Archie. "I walked past your sister Maggie and she was with the old dear. I wouldn't have known it was her if they hadn't been together, but I did a double take and realised who it was. As I say, she'd aged well, although she didn't look happy."

"She was never happy." Mr Watson clenched his drink.

"Is that why you parted ways with her?" Eliza asked.

Mr Watson emptied his glass. "You could say that."

Eliza stood up and paced to the window and back. "Something's puzzling me. If you all left the bar at the same time, and Mr Burns spent the afternoon with Mr Watson, how is it that only Mr Burns saw the two Mrs Scotts?"

Mr Watson studied his neighbour. "You went home for something, didn't you?"

"I did, those papers. I nipped in and picked them up, and

it was when I came out that I saw the two of them. Mr Watson would have reached Clifftop House by then."

"And what about the rest of you?"

Mr Cargill's features slumped. "And as I said, I could have walked past her and wouldn't have noticed. More's the pity."

"You were with me, if you remember." Mr Stewart smoothed down his moustache. "You didn't miss anything."

Mr Dowie frowned at Mr McKay. "Why didn't we see them?"

Mr McKay stared at his tankard before pointing at his friend. "We called at the shop before we went back to the beach. You wanted some tobacco."

Mr Dowie nodded. "You're right, I did. That's a shame, I'd have liked to see her again."

"And you didn't see anyone else after you left here?" Eliza asked.

"There was someone hanging around the church," Mr Watson said.

"You saw him?"

"You mean someone else has already told you about him?"

"Possibly. We've had another report of a stranger being in the village." Eliza sat down and retrieved her pencil. "Could you describe him?"

Mr Watson paused. "About my height but not the same build. Rather thin, actually; his jacket looked too big for him ... and he had dark hair that was greying around the edges."

"It sounds like the same man. What time did you see him?"

"Once I got home. I was wondering where Mr Burns was and so I looked out of the front window. The chap saw me and immediately disappeared into the graveyard." Mr Watson scowled.

"So you didn't speak to him?"

"Why would I?"

"No reason." Eliza turned to Mr Burns. "Did you see him, too?"

Mr Burns shook his head. "Not properly. I might have seen the back of him as he disappeared into the churchyard, but I couldn't tell you anything about him, he was too far away."

"All right, that's something. At least it confirms the reports of a man being outside the church on Thursday."

"Have you spoken to the minister?" Mr Burns asked.

"We have, but he hadn't seen anyone new to the village."

"Perhaps he knew him." Mr Watson's comment stopped Eliza with her pencil poised above her notepad.

"That's a very good point. Just because he was a stranger to you, doesn't mean he was to the reverend. We need to go back and check with him."

Archie was on his feet again. "Thank you, gentleman, that's enough for one day. We won't take up any more of your time."

"May I ask a question?" Henry jumped up, stopping his father where he was. "I need to leave in five minutes, but I wondered if anyone knew that Mrs Scott had plans to move back to St Giles."

"She was moving back!" Mr Burns stared at his friends. "Did any of you know?"

"I don't think the family knew, never mind the rest of us." Mr Stewart's eyes narrowed as he stared at Henry. "Are you sure?"

"Yes, we are," Eliza said. "She'd instructed a solicitor to sell her house in Cupar."

"That doesn't mean she'd move here."

Eliza's eyes narrowed. "Where else would she go? I wasn't aware she had family anywhere else."

"None of us are in a position to confirm or deny that." Mr Watson glanced around his friends. "As we've said, except for the brief glimpse Mr Burns had of her on Thursday, nobody here had laid eyes on her in over twenty years."

Eliza sighed. "All right, I'll need to check that. I'd just assumed she'd want to come here to be with her son."

Mr Stewart shook his head. "I doubt it. She only wanted Robert to be her handyman; he told me once she didn't care about him."

"Mr Scott wouldn't have been happy about her coming back given the way she treated him." Mr Watson pushed his glass across the bar for another Scotch. "Nor his missus for that matter."

"It would have made life easier for him, though," Mr Burns said.

Mr Stewart cleared his throat. "Only because he wouldn't have to travel to Cupar so often. Her living here would bring its own problems, probably more than it solved."

"If you want my opinion, they've had a fortunate escape." There was no hint of emotion on Mr Watson's face. "They should be thanking whoever did it."

"Really, gentlemen, that's no way to speak of the dead." Connie's voice squeaked as she spoke.

"No, I'm sorry." Mr Watson spun his glass on the bar.

"No apology needed." Eliza reached down for her handbag. "I think that will be all for now. Thank you for your time." With a faint smile at Connie, she strode over to Archie and linked her arm through his. "Shall we go?"

The scowl on Archie's face when they got outside convinced Eliza that she needed to send him off to his parents' house.

"He's not very pleased with me." She pulled her lips tight as she watched him leave with Henry.

"Well, he should be. You found out a lot while we were there."

"Maybe, but we still don't know anyone with a strong enough motive for wanting her dead."

"Other than Mr and Mrs Scott, you mean?"

Eliza grimaced. "Yes, except for them."

Connie looked up and down the street. "What will we do now? Should we go and ask Mr Scott about the telegram he didn't send?"

"Hmm, we could, but we've a few things to mull over and it might be worth letting him think he's fooled us for the time being."

"What about the reverend? We could go back to the manse."

Eliza gazed towards the sea glistening in the sunshine. "Why don't we take a walk. It's Sunday tomorrow so I expect we'll be going to church. We can speak to him then. I don't suppose he knows much, anyway."

CHAPTER TWELVE

The church wasn't big, and although half the village were reportedly on holiday, Eliza and Connie had to squeeze onto the end of a pew near the back of the nave, while Archie and Henry sat behind them.

"At least the reverend has a few more candles lit this morning." Eliza straightened her skirt as she sat down. "I'd forgotten what it's like to rely on them. You'd think they'd at least have gas lamps by now."

"Perhaps they don't want them. There is something special about having a service by candlelight." Connie glanced at the woman sitting to her left before lowering her voice. "What will you do if we've not found the ... *murderer* ... by Saturday?"

"We'll have to leave it to the police, I suppose, which means we need to make sure we do find them..."

Her sentence was cut short as the organist struck up the chords for the first hymn. Eliza stood up, her hymn book open at the right page, but she had no urge to sing; instead, she studied the congregation around her. The fishermen she'd met the previous day looked much smarter as they sat with their wives two rows in front of them. Mr Watson and Mr Burns sat together behind the Thomsons, who needed three pews to accommodate the whole family.

"Have you seen anything of interest?" Connie whispered as they retook their seats.

"No, nothing at all, but I can't help thinking there's someone here who knows what happened."

"I don't suppose you can speak to all of them."

Eliza eyed those around her. "No, probably not."

By the time the minister recited the final prayer, Eliza was ready to go.

"Aren't you going to wait and speak to the reverend?" Connie asked as they stood up.

"Yes, of course, I just wish we could wait outside. I've had enough of being in such a dark and dreary place."

"Well, hopefully it'll be worth it; he may be able to suggest the best people to talk to."

Eliza stepped into the aisle to let out the family sitting beside them before she was forced back into the pew as those seated closer to the front pushed past. "I certainly hope so."

"Come this way." Connie pointed to the other end of the pew where they could stand in the side aisle. "We can look around, there are some nice things down here."

Eliza peered into an alcove and studied a bronze statue of Christ on the cross. "It's a shame you can't see these very well from the pews. The light doesn't reach the back of the recesses."

"There's something in each of them." Connie walked down the side of the church, stopping every few feet to admire another statue. "You'd see the detail better if they placed candles in each."

"They wouldn't want to spend the money on them. Remember when we called the other day, there were only about three candles lit. It's not a very welcoming place."

"No, you're right." Connie nodded towards the door. "We can probably go now, most people have left."

Eliza led the way. "Good morning, Reverend." She gave him her best smile as he took her hand. "A lovely service."

"How kind; I don't get many compliments from the locals. They've heard my views on most aspects of the Bible more times than they'd care to admit."

Connie took his hand. "I'm sure that's not true."

The smile dropped from the minister's face. "I'm afraid it is. I've been here so long I remember even the most elderly villager when they were a child."

Eliza studied him. "How long would that be?"

"Most of my life. I moved from St Andrews for my probationary year and originally planned to go back, but a month before my time was complete, Reverend Campbell died. I supported the congregation during the aftermath, and after a period of reflection, they ordained me to minister here. I've been here ever since."

"So you'll remember Mrs Scott from when she lived here?"

The minister nodded, his eyes glazing over at the memory. "Miss Davison she was then. Such a tragedy what happened to her." His attention suddenly returned to Eliza. "I had the police here yesterday."

"Really? Were they making enquiries into the death?"

"They mentioned it was suspicious and asked what I'd

been doing on Thursday." The minister held his hands together in front of his chest. "I told them the same as I told you, that I'd been in the garden."

Eliza nodded. "Did they say anything else?"

"Only that we can't arrange the funeral yet."

"I imagine that will be because they've not had the results of the post-mortem. Hopefully, we'll hear something this week." Eliza cleared her throat. "Do you mind if I ask you another question? Since we last spoke, we've had a couple of people mention that they saw a stranger loitering around the church. You said you didn't see anyone on Thursday, but I wonder if you'd seen him at any other time."

The minister shook his head. "I don't recall seeing anyone I don't know, but if you could describe what he looks like..."

Eliza took the notepaper from her handbag and read the details.

"That's not a stranger, it sounds like Mr Carmichael."

"You know him?"

"Yes, I've known him all his life."

A frown settled on Eliza's face. "In that case, how is it that the villagers who saw him hadn't seen him before?"

"Ah, he's not from around here. He's from St Andrews and I often see him if I'm at the church down there."

"Have you any idea why he might have been here this week?"

The minister stiffened and stared out towards the sea. "Well, it wouldn't be to kill Mrs Scott, if that's what you're implying. He's a perfect gentleman."

"Good gracious, no; please forgive me. I wouldn't suggest he's our murderer without knowing more about him but ... well, he was reported as acting strangely."

"In what way?"

"According to several people he was hanging around outside the church and when he realised he'd been seen he came into the churchyard to look at the gravestones."

"I'd hardly call that unusual behaviour." The minister's face hardened. "Many people take a great deal of comfort from visiting graves."

Connie nodded. "You're right; I'm often at peace when I visit my late husband's grave."

Eliza softened her tone. "So does he come here because his parents are buried here ... or a wife, perhaps?"

"No, not at all. He never married and his parents are from St Andrews, so they're buried down there. No, unfortunately he's not had an easy life and so taking an hour to wander around the graves may be what he needs to calm his soul." The minister paused. "Now, if you'll excuse me, I need to blow the candles out."

Eliza grimaced as Reverend Rennie left them. "That didn't exactly go to plan." She linked her arm through Connie's as they headed back to the road.

"You weren't to know."

"No, it's interesting, though, don't you think, that he's been here all his working life."

"And that he knew Mrs Scott long before she was married."

Eliza gazed over to the sea, the sun rippling across the waves. "I imagine there's not much goes on in the village he doesn't hear about. Perhaps we just need to work out the right questions to ask."

Archie and Henry were waiting for them when they

arrived at the inn, and Archie made a point of taking his pocket watch from his waistcoat.

"Nice of you to come back; I was beginning to think you weren't coming."

"Don't be like that." Eliza walked through to the dining room, thankful that none of the other tables were occupied. "We needed to talk to Reverend Rennie, and you seemed rather preoccupied with your mother."

Henry held out a chair for her. "What did you want to ask him?"

"About the stranger." Connie took the seat Archie offered her. "Although he's not a stranger."

"He's not?" Henry's eyes were wide. "Who is he then?"

"Someone called Mr Carmichael. Apparently, he's from St Andrews but the reverend's known him for years and said he's a real gentleman."

"Did you get an address so we can go and visit him?" Henry asked.

"Unfortunately not." Eliza adjusted a napkin on her lap. "The reverend was a bit annoyed when we suggested it was unusual for anyone to want to spend time in the graveyard and made his apologies to leave. I'll give it a day or two and then visit him again."

Eliza waited while four plates of roast beef and vegetables were placed on the table before she rested a hand on Archie's. "Why didn't you tell me you knew the reverend?"

Archie shrugged. "It didn't occur to me. Does it matter?"

"I'm not sure, but it might be useful. Mrs Scott hadn't lived here for over twenty years and yet he remembered her, too."

"And is that relevant?" Archie removed his hand and picked up his knife.

"Who knows? The thing is, someone wanted her dead and I can't help wondering if it's because she was coming back to St Giles. If that's the case, there must be a reason she left in the first place."

"You mean that by coming back she's opened some old wounds?" Henry asked.

"Precisely."

"But who knew she was even here?" Archie sliced into a boiled potato. "I didn't think anyone knew outside of the family."

"And that's the problem." Eliza put down her knife and fork. "What was the reverend like when you used to live here?"

Archie shrugged. "Like a minister. He's not changed really, other than his hair's gone white and he has more wrinkles. I even have a feeling I've heard this morning's sermon before."

"Hmm." Eliza stabbed a carrot. "There's something here that doesn't add up. I just wish I could work out what it is."

"Are you visiting anyone this afternoon?" Henry asked.

"It's difficult on a Sunday." She looked at Archie. "What are you doing?"

"I promised Ma I'd call."

Eliza turned to Henry. "Are you going, too?"

"I'm going to see Rabbie and Callum. They leave on Tuesday and I don't know when I'll see them again."

"Could we visit Mr and Mrs Scott?" Connie asked. "They are family and so it's not like calling on villagers we don't know."

"Yes, that's an excellent idea." Eliza attacked the rest of her food with renewed vigour. "I want to understand more about Mrs Scott's past. I'm sure there's something we should know."

"And we need to ask about the telegram."

Eliza dabbed her lips with her napkin. "We do indeed."

CHAPTER THIRTEEN

It looked as if the remaining villagers were taking advantage of the last days of summer as Archie walked Eliza and Connie to the Scotts' house.

"I've not seen so many people out at once since we arrived." Eliza smiled to an elderly couple who passed them on their way to the beach.

Archie laughed. "It's Sunday afternoon; it's about the only time most of them get to themselves."

"Well, they've got a lovely day for it." Connie watched the pair as they stepped onto the sand. "We could walk along the beach once we've finished here."

"That sounds nice."

"I'll join you." Archie escorted them across the road but stopped on the corner near his sister's house. "I won't come in with you or else I'll never get away, but give me an hour and I'll be back."

"While you're at your ma and pa's, will you ask them what they remember about Mrs Scott when she was young. I'm sure they'll have known her, but they won't speak to me."

Archie sighed. "If I must. I'll see you later."

Eliza watched Archie leave before she knocked on Maggie's door and pushed it open.

"May we come in?"

Maggie was at the kitchen sink, her face pale as she offered them a weak smile. "Yes, take a seat. There's tea in the pot."

"Are you on your own?" Eliza asked.

"Robert's nipped outside. He'll be back in a minute. The girls have gone for a walk."

"You're very fortunate having such a lovely place to walk," Connie said. "We can stroll around our village in about twenty minutes and that's it."

"Don't forget the duck pond at one end; who needs the sea when you've got that." Eliza chuckled as she poured milk into two cups. "Do you want one, Maggie?"

"Ooh, yes, please. I've been washing up for half an hour ... you'd better pour one for Robert, too."

With four cups of milky tea steaming in the middle of the table, Maggie wiped her hands on a towel and sat down.

"How are you feeling?" Eliza asked.

Maggie put two heaped spoonfuls of sugar into her cup. "Tired mainly. I've not slept since the police suggested I could be the killer. They won't arrest me, will they?"

Who knows? Eliza forced a smile to her lips. "Let's not give them the chance."

"The sooner you find out who did it the better." Maggie's eyes suddenly brightened. "You've not found them, have you?"

"Unfortunately, not, although I do have a few thoughts I'd like to discuss with you and Mr Scott."

119

Maggie took a sip of her tea. "He won't be long."

As if on cue, the door in the far corner of the room opened and Mr Scott sauntered in and sat down at the table. "Good afternoon, ladies. I thought I heard voices."

"Good afternoon, Mr Scott. How are you today?" Connie smiled sweetly.

His shoulders sagged. "Not too bad, all things considered. Have you made any progress finding the killer?"

"No, not really, although I can't help thinking that all of this is connected to the fact Mrs Scott planned on moving back." Eliza put down her cup.

"But how could it? Nobody knew." Mr Scott's brow creased.

"No one in the family, but somebody must have known." Eliza held Mr Scott's gaze. "Can you tell me anything about why she left St Giles?"

Mr Scott shook his head. "Nothing that makes sense."

"She announced it on our wedding day." Maggie gazed at her ornate china cup as she fidgeted with the teaspoon.

Eliza did a double take. "On the day you were married! How long ago was that?"

"Twenty-five years. She told us at the wedding breakfast, and within the week she'd gone."

"Didn't that seem out of character?"

Maggie stared at Eliza with tears in eyes. "Nothing she did seemed unusual, just nasty. She made the villagers believe it was because she didn't like me."

"And was it true?"

Maggie shrugged. "We didn't get on very well, but it wasn't so bad that she needed to leave ... at least not in my opinion."

Eliza paused. "What about you, Mr Scott? Did you ever ask her why she was going?"

"Oh yes, I asked her, but I got a different answer." Mr Scott's nostrils flared as he pushed himself up from the table to pace the kitchen. "She told me it was because I didn't need her any more. Pa was quite a bully when I was young and she'd always stood up for me, but because I'd chosen to get married and move here, she decided to go with Pa."

"So it was your father who wanted to go? Could that be the real reason she moved, because he told her to?"

Mr Scott stared at the table. "Possibly, although I doubt it. She never did anything she didn't want to, not even when Pa ordered her to."

"Tell me–" Eliza studied him "–how long has he been dead?"

"Only since the start of this year, January. Not that I was sorry. I was glad to see the back of him, but once the funeral was over, I realised Ma would be more reliant on me."

"So that's when you started going to Cupar more regularly, to help her with the croft."

"She didn't need me for that." Mr Scott sat down again, his fingers restless on the table. "There were always hired hands to manage the sheep, even when Pa was alive. She did it out of spite, to make life difficult for me."

Eliza exchanged glances with Connie. "But why would she do that? You were her only son."

Mr Scott threw his hands in the air. "You would wonder, wouldn't you? If you want my opinion, it was because it gave her a feeling of power. Something she'd never had before."

"Could it have been because your pa died that she decided to move back here?"

"As I say, it could have been, but I doubt it."

"So you can't think of any reason why she'd want to come back?"

"No, nothing."

"She was up to something." Maggie's eyes narrowed. "And perhaps someone found out what it was and realised they had to stop her."

Connie placed her cup back on its saucer. "It must have been something terrible if it was worth killing her over."

"You'd think so..." Eliza paused "... although, I wonder... Could her death have been down to a robbery that went wrong? Her purse was missing from her bag when we found it."

"If that was the case, why kill her?" Connie asked.

Eliza shrugged. "Maybe she recognised her assailants and they couldn't risk her reporting them to the police."

Mr Scott once again stood up. "It seems rather drastic, strangling her before throwing her from the cliff. I mean, if it was a robbery, a simple push would have been enough."

"I suspect you're right, although the drop to the beach isn't terribly high. Maybe they wanted to be certain she was dead." Eliza's unused pencil hovered over her paper.

"Do you have a description of the purse?" Connie asked. "Perhaps we could look for it."

Maggie screwed up her face. "Now, that's a question. I hadn't seen it for a while, with her only just arriving, but last time I saw it, it was brown leather edged with silver mounts. They were quite ornate on the corners."

"I know the ones you mean." Connie smiled. "They're rather nice. I'm sure we'll recognise it if we see it."

The room fell silent, and Eliza became aware of the tick-tock from the grandfather clock in the hallway. She glanced at Mr Scott as he approached the far wall of the kitchen. *Do I ask him with Maggie here? Yes. We need an answer.* She bit down on her lip.

"Mr Scott, I'm sorry to ask you this, but you told us that on the afternoon of the murder you sent a telegram; that was how you met Maggie when she was looking for your ma."

Mr Scott turned slowly to face her. "Y-yes."

"Well, the thing is, Mr and Mrs Baker confirmed that neither of them sent a telegram for you, or anyone else for that matter. Can you explain that?"

"Did I say send a telegram?" Mr Scott gave a nervous laugh. "What was I thinking? I meant to say post a letter."

Eliza stared at him as his face grew redder. "A letter. Can I ask who to?"

"Well, no, not to post a letter. To ask if there was anything waiting for me."

"From what I've seen, the postman calls at least twice a day. Was it so urgent that you needed to pick it up?"

Mr Scott's eyes flicked between Eliza and Maggie.

"What are you hiding?" Maggie jumped to her feet.

"Nothing, honestly." Mr Scott edged away towards the back door. "If you must know, I wondered what had happened to Maggie and Ma. They'd only gone to the shop, or at least that's what they'd told me, and when they hadn't come back three quarters of an hour later, I was concerned. They'd argued before they left the house..."

"So you *do* think I killed her." Maggie's nostrils flared. "That's why you were so angry with me when we met. You've thought it was me all along."

"No ... not really. I prayed it wasn't you..."

"And that's supposed to make me feel better?" Maggie's eyes were wild as she glared at her husband. "I've done nothing wrong." She grabbed Eliza's hands. "You believe me, don't you?"

"I've said all along that I didn't think a woman was capable of doing it."

"There you are." She turned back to her husband. "Eliza's been here for less than a week and she knows me better than you do."

"What did you expect me to think?" Mr Scott stayed by the door. "You were the last person to see her alive and wanted to send her home again within ten minutes of her arriving."

Eliza nodded. She couldn't argue with that, but she stood up and put an arm around her sister-in-law. "Maggie, Mr Scott, please come and sit down. I didn't mean to cause an argument."

The two of them exchanged glances before Mr Scott nodded. "It's just been such a shock; I didn't want Maggie getting the blame ... honestly."

Eliza kept her voice level. "And she won't, not if we all tell the truth and keep no secrets."

Maggie took a mouthful of her now cold tea. "The problem is, we've no idea what Ma was up to. She never told us anything."

"I can believe that." Eliza pursed her lips as she pondered her next question. "Mr Scott, did you know your ma was once walking out with Mr Watson?"

Mr Scott blinked rapidly as he studied her. "Mr Watson from Clifftop House? No. When?"

"Many years ago, before she married your pa."

Mr Scott shook his head. "I'd no idea..."

"I don't suppose she'd have wanted us to know." Maggie reached out a hand to her husband.

Eliza nodded. "You're probably right. I just wondered if you were aware of the friendship. When Mr Cargill mentioned it to us, I got the impression your ma had left him rather abruptly."

Mr Scott's head jerked up. "Mr Cargill knew?"

"By the sounds of it, most of the older folk in the village did; they were all young men and women together and your mother was one of their friends."

Mr Scott let out a loud rasp. "I'm sorry, but this is all news to me. The fact that Ma changed her mind about being with him doesn't surprise me, though. She was a law unto herself."

"But you're not aware of any contact between her and any of the men in the village while she was in Cupar?"

"No, none. It was almost as if she tried to forget that St Giles existed. I kept her up to date with the news, but she rarely listened. She only took an interest in things that affected her."

"Such as?"

Mr Scott drummed his fingers on the table. "I can't think now. She was always asking if any of the older villagers had died, but I put that down to the fact she had a morbid curiosity."

"Was she interested in anyone in particular?"

He shook his head. "Not that I remember."

Eliza sighed. "It was only a thought. We're no closer to finding a motive for anyone, and until we do, it's difficult to prove Maggie's innocence."

"You will keep trying though ... won't you?" Maggie's blue

eyes welled with tears again. "I'm frightened the police will just turn up and arrest me."

"Don't worry, we won't let it get to that." Eliza wished she felt as confident as she sounded, but her smile returned when she heard Archie at the front door.

Maggie jumped from her chair and wiped her eyes before turning to the sink. "Let me put the kettle on again. We could all do with another cup of tea."

CHAPTER FOURTEEN

The following morning, the sun shone brightly from a pastel blue sky, untroubled by the wisps of clouds around it.

"Another lovely day." Connie closed her eyes and took a deep breath as she stood on the doorstep to the inn. "It's such a shame we can't go for a longer walk."

"You can if you hurry up." Archie offered his arm to Eliza before they set off for the opposite side of the village. "Not too much chattering."

Eliza gave him a sideways glance. "There's chatting and there's fact-finding. I like to think we're doing the latter, unlike you with your ma and pa. I don't believe they know nothing about Mrs Scott, given she was their daughter's mother-in-law."

"That's what they said, and I could hardly accuse them of lying."

"There are ways of asking questions and you've clearly not got the knack." Eliza scowled. "The thing troubling me, is that the villagers seem to be hiding something, but unless they start being honest with us, we won't be able to prove Maggie's innocence. Why would anyone want to pin the blame on her?"

Archie shook his head. "I don't think anyone's doing it deliberately, it's just that people don't believe Mrs Scott's past has anything to do with it."

"But why wouldn't they? And even if you're right, it wouldn't do them any harm to tell us what happened; if it has no bearing on the case, it won't go any further."

"Maybe they don't trust us to keep our counsel. It's a small village, even I'm an outsider now and they barely know you."

Eliza nodded. "You could be right. I suppose it would be different if we were still in Moreton." She paused and peered down the road that bent away to the right as it hugged the coastline. "How far do the houses go?"

"They're rather spread out from here, but I'd suggest you start at the one over there." Archie pointed to a neat single-storey house on the left with views out across the sea.

Eliza glanced around her. "Why? Because you can see the bench from there? Don't you think we'd be better walking a little further in case anyone spotted Mr Carmichael?"

"I suggest you do that later if you need to, but I've brought you here for a reason." There was a twinkle in Archie's eyes. "The lady who lives here is familiar with almost everyone in the village and is of a similar nature to Moreton's Mrs Petty."

Eliza's eyes lit up. "Really! St Giles has its own old lady who sits in the window watching the world go by? What's her name?"

Archie laughed. "That's one way of putting it. Her name's Miss McGovern and she's probably got her eyes on us now."

"Oh, how exciting. We need something to get this investigation going. Why didn't you bring us here sooner?"

"We've not had a lot of time. Now, I'll leave you to speak to her, but shall I do the introductions before I go?" Archie asked.

Eliza nodded. "Yes, please. It won't do any harm to have her thinking she's helping the doctor from London."

Archie escorted Eliza and Connie up the short garden path and knocked on the front door. It was opened by an elderly woman with light grey hair, wearing a formal navy gown that gave the image of a prim Victorian hostess of ten years earlier. Her watery blue eyes shone as Archie made the introductions.

"How splendid to meet you." She ushered them inside as Archie bade them farewell. "Come on in and I'll put the kettle on."

Eliza and Connie took the offered seats in the centre of a large bay window that overlooked the headland and the sea beyond.

"What a splendid view. It's clear why she spends hours sitting here," Connie said. "And you can see the bench."

Eliza sat to the left of Connie and leaned forward towards the window. "I suspect there's a reason why Miss McGovern sits on this side. You get a better view of the headland from here and the goings-on around the church."

"Here we are." Miss McGovern rejoined them and placed a large tea tray on the table in front of them. "I'm not in the habit of receiving visitors and so this is a pleasant surprise."

"What a marvellous view you have." Eliza indicated towards the sea.

"Yes, it's lovely at this time of the year, although it does get

129

rather desolate in the winter. I don't suppose you'll make the journey outside of the summer months."

"I doubt it." Eliza watched Miss McGovern pour the tea, her hair fixed neatly under her summer bonnet.

"There we are." She placed three cups and saucers on the table. "Now, what may I do for you?"

"I presume you've heard about the death of Mrs Scott," Eliza started.

"Oh yes. What a terrible thing for a village like this. Have the police found out what happened?"

Eliza shook her head. "Not to my knowledge, but the family are concerned that the killer could be living amongst us and we need to find them."

"Well, of course."

Eliza again glanced out of the window. "Did you see anything unusual on Thursday afternoon last week? I don't imagine much gets past you from here."

Miss McGovern chuckled. "Not much, and I did see something as it happens." She gave them a knowing look. "There was a man I hadn't seen before wandering up and down the road."

"Really!" Eliza's eyes widened as she reached in her bag for her pencil and paper. "We've already had sightings of a stranger, but we don't know enough about him yet. Could you describe him?"

"Well, he was a strange-looking fellow. Rather thin and wearing a jacket that looked too big for him."

"That's him!" Connie all but bounced in her seat.

Eliza nodded. "There are similarities, but let's be sure. Do you remember anything else, Miss McGovern?"

"He was probably around fifty years old; I would say. His

hair was starting to grey, but you could tell it had once been dark ... and he had very shifty eyes."

"You were that close to him?"

"Unfortunately, yes. I was here with my knitting when he walked past the window towards St Giles. I didn't get a good look at him at the time because he had his back to me before I noticed him."

"When would that have been?" Eliza asked.

"Now, it was Thursday, but it was during that indeterminate time between lunch and afternoon tea. Probably around quarter past two, maybe a little earlier."

"And you saw him again?"

"I did. It must have been over an hour later he came back looking rather flustered."

"Flustered!" Connie's eyes were wide.

Miss McGovern gave a deliberate nod of the head. "Exactly. Not only that, he stopped by the hedge and appeared to be studying the house." She gave a dramatic shudder. "It was quite unnerving I can tell you."

Connie put her hands to her mouth. "How awful."

"What happened then?" Eliza asked.

"Well, he was looking at the house, but as soon as he realised I was watching him, he put his head down and hurried away."

"And what time do you think that was?"

Miss McGovern paused to think. "I'd just made a cup of tea, so probably five past or ten past three."

"So that was on the day of the murder." Eliza made a note on her paper. "Have you seen him since?"

Another deliberate nod. "On Friday morning. I got up at eight o'clock as usual and when I opened the curtains at around half past eight, there he was, as large as life, staring at me!"

Connie gasped. "What did you do?"

"As soon as I saw him, I pulled them closed again, but after about five minutes I found the courage to take a peek through them."

"And was he still there?"

"He was sitting on the bench across the road, staring out to sea."

Connie put a hand on Eliza's knee. "Perhaps he was contemplating what he'd done."

"It's possible, but highly unlikely. Would he really have come back if he'd been responsible?" Eliza stared across to the bench.

"Oh my goodness, you know what that means, don't you?" Connie's shriek brought Eliza's attention back to the room. "While we were on the beach with the body, he was above us on the headland. He might have watched everything."

It was Eliza's turn to shudder. "You're right. We probably didn't miss him by much when we came up here."

"That may not have been accidental," Miss McGovern said. "He could have seen you walking from the beach and known you were heading towards him."

Eliza swivelled in her chair. "On the day of the murder, did you see where he went?"

Miss McGovern sighed. "I'm afraid I didn't. One of the drawbacks of living here is that it's so close to the bend you can't see around it."

Connie stared at Eliza. "He could have gone into the churchyard again and watched us from there. He may even have seen us this morning as we came here."

"All right, let's not get carried away." Eliza paused. "Miss McGovern, what else can you tell us? Did you see Mrs Scott on Thursday?"

"I did, although I didn't realise it was her at the time. I hadn't seen her for years and didn't recognise her. I just saw Maggie Scott, helping an elderly lady to the bench before she disappeared off back around the bend."

"That would be to go to the shop," Connie said.

"Did Mrs Scott talk to anyone once Maggie had disappeared?"

Miss McGovern shook her head. "No. She hadn't been on her own for more than a minute when she got up and hurried around the bend herself. I presumed she was going after Maggie, but *Maggie* came back about twenty minutes later as if she was looking for something."

"Or someone." Connie gave Eliza a knowing look.

"How did Maggie seem when she came back?"

"Well, it's interesting you should ask. She was rather frantic, turning this way and that as if she'd lost something before she headed towards St Andrews. She can't have gone far because she was back again ten or fifteen minutes later."

"Does that give Maggie an alibi?" Connie asked.

Eliza sucked on the end of her pencil. "I wish it did, but I don't think so. Miss McGovern couldn't know what happened when they both disappeared around the bend, so, theoretically at least, Maggie could have killed Mrs Scott while she was out of view and then gone to the bench pretending to look for her. She may have hoped Miss McGovern was watching so it would give her an alibi." Eliza paused and flicked through her notes. "Where does the stranger fit into all this? You said he was here before quarter past two. Had Mrs Scott left the bench by then?"

"Now you mention it, she had, although I did notice the man studying the seat as he walked towards it."

"But he just kept on walking?"

"I'm afraid so."

"Didn't Mr Watson say he'd seen him?" Connie asked. "That would confirm the time he left the inn."

"He did. He also said the man went into the churchyard."

"Which could explain why no one else saw him." Connie nodded to herself. "I imagine it's quite easy to hide amongst the gravestones."

Eliza put down her pencil and stared at the sea. "Despite everything we know, I still feel as if we're missing something. Miss McGovern, were you on good terms with Mrs Scott when she lived here?"

"Not particularly. In a village this size, everyone knows everyone else, but we weren't friends. More acquaintances, I would say."

"Could you tell us anything about her?"

Miss McGovern paused as if searching for the right words. "I shouldn't be saying this under the circumstances, but ... if I'm being honest, I didn't like the woman. I spoke to her on occasion, but tried to stay out of her way."

Eliza cocked her head. "What didn't you like about her?"

"It's hard to put my finger on it, but she was just one of those women who knew how to upset you. She was always a little too personal and would use it to her advantage."

"Did she have any close friends?"

"Oh yes, the men couldn't see enough of her. She didn't tease them the way she did us. We'd often say the men were like bees around a honey pot when she was about. Not that it did her much good in the end."

"What do you mean?"

"Well, running off with Mr Scott the way she did and ending up in the middle of nowhere. Don't tell me she was happy doing that, because I won't believe you."

"That's interesting." Eliza's brow furrowed. "Have you any idea why she might have gone?"

Miss McGovern paused as a police carriage pulled up outside. "No, I've no idea. As I said, we weren't on the best of terms, I was just glad to see her go."

Eliza shot a glance to Connie. "What on earth are they doing here? Please, Miss McGovern, we'd rather you didn't mention that we were asking about Mrs Scott. They get a bit tetchy."

Miss McGovern chuckled. "They don't want any help then. Trust me, I won't say a word." She excused herself as the police knocked on the front door. A moment later, she led them into the living room.

"Mrs Thomson, Mrs Appleton. Getting to know the locals, are you?" The sergeant held his cap under his arm as the constable hovered behind him.

"Yes, we've had rather a pleasant time, thank you." Eliza pursed her lips. "What brings you here? Is it to do with Mrs Scott's death?"

"It is, as it happens. I hope you're not here for the same reason. Murder investigations are for the police to deal with."

"So, it's a murder investigation now?" Eliza feigned surprise. "I wasn't aware you were treating it as such. Do you have the results of the post-mortem?"

"If we have, it's no concern of yours. Now, if you wouldn't

mind giving us a few minutes with Miss McGovern. We have a few questions for her."

Eliza bent down to pick up her bag. "Yes, of course, we were just on our way out." She headed towards the door but stopped. "Can I ask how you're getting on with your enquiries? Have you been able to eliminate Maggie Scott from your list of suspects yet?"

"As I say, that's no concern..."

Eliza smiled. "Actually, Sergeant, it is. Maggie Scott's my husband's sister and so the whole family are rather anxious to know what happened to the elderly Mrs Scott. If you have any information, I'm sure they'd appreciate it. Can I inform them that the cause of death has been recorded as strangulation?"

The sergeant's cheeks coloured. "How did you know that?"

Eliza stepped back towards him. "I imagine that's why it's now a murder investigation rather than the accident you initially thought."

The sergeant's smile faded. "If you put it like that, yes, she did die of strangulation."

"Which suggests a man is more likely to be the killer." She nodded her head, but the sergeant failed to follow suit.

"A woman could just as easily have pushed the body from the cliff as a man, especially if she was working with someone."

Eliza nodded. "That's true, although I doubt she could have thrown it that far from the headland. It would need a man to do that." She pulled open the door for Connie. "Anyway, thank you for the tea, Miss McGovern. It was really nice talking to you."

CHAPTER FIFTEEN

Eliza and Connie stepped out of the front door and hurried down the garden path before turning right towards the village.

"Gosh, that was close." Eliza glanced back at Miss McGovern's window to see the police officers sitting in the seats they'd occupied not five minutes earlier. "At least they've realised it was murder."

"But they've not discounted Maggie, have they?"

Eliza opened up her parasol to shield them from the sergeant's gaze. "No, they seem more determined than ever to find her guilty. Hopefully, they'll come to their senses before we leave."

"But what about the stranger, Mr Carmichael? It looks like he should be high on our list of suspects."

"You'd think so, although the police probably don't know about him yet. I imagine Miss McGovern will mention him."

"I wonder if they've found out anything we haven't."

"I doubt it, but now they've got the results of the post-mortem, they may have spoken to Archie. Maybe he can tell us more over luncheon."

Archie and Henry were already seated in the dining room when they returned, and much to Eliza's annoyance, so were half a dozen others.

"Have you had a good morning?" Archie stood up and held out a seat for each of them.

"Not bad, although we were cut short by the police. Have they been to see you this morning?"

Archie gave Eliza a sideways glance. "No, why? What are they up to?"

She leaned forward with a whisper. "They've had the result of the post-mortem; the cause of death was strangulation."

"Ah, so they've started a murder enquiry?"

"It looks like it, but they still seem to have Maggie in their sights."

Archie groaned. "I need to have a word with them. Didn't you find out anything that might help?"

"I'm afraid not, other than someone needs to straighten out that bend in the road. It's amazing what Miss McGovern misses because of it."

Archie grinned. "I'm afraid I can't do anything about that, but Henry might have something to cheer you up."

"Really?" Eliza raised an eyebrow to her son. "What have you been up to?"

With a large grin on his face, Henry reached into his jacket pocket and pulled out a brown leather purse with silverwork on the corners. "What do you think of that?"

Connie clapped her hands together. "It's Mrs Scott's."

Eliza nudged her. "Keep your voice down!"

Connie's cheeks coloured as she lowered her voice. "I'm sorry, but this is so exciting. Where did you find it?"

Henry didn't take his eyes off his mother. "It's Rabbie and Callum's last day today, so we decided to go for a stroll around the churchyard."

Eliza shuddered. "Were you hoping to find Mr Carmichael by any chance?"

One corner of Henry's mouth curled up. "Perhaps, but when he wasn't there, we decided to see if he'd left any clues behind."

"Did you find anything else?"

Henry wrinkled his nose. "No, and we nearly missed this. We walked around the graves, right up to the top, but when we found nothing we returned to the church and this was near the back wall."

Eliza picked it up. "Have you looked through it?"

"We had a quick look but didn't touch anything. I thought you'd want to do that."

Eliza flashed him a smile. "Thank you." She was about to open it when a plate of kedgeree was put down in front of her. "Ah." She slipped the purse into her handbag. "I suppose we'd better eat first. I'm sure another five minutes won't hurt."

With four clean plates neatly stacked, Eliza retrieved the purse. "Let's see what we've got here." She rifled through an assortment of papers before arranging them on the table. "Well, there's no money for a start."

"No, we noticed that. It just looked like a collection of waste paper."

Eliza studied a number of handwritten receipts before she spotted a neatly folded piece of paper with two addresses on it.

"What is it?" Connie leaned across the table to get a better view. "Addresses?"

"Yes, but not just any addresses, or at least not the first one. It's for Clifftop House." Her eyes narrowed as she looked to Archie sitting beside her. "That's where Mr Watson lives. Her old beau. Why would she have his address on a piece of paper?"

Archie's face was blank. "I've no idea." He leaned across to look at the other address. "Who does that belong to?"

Eliza shrugged. "You're the one from around here."

"I'm from St Giles, not St Andrews. Why would she have a St Andrews address?"

"Are there any names?" Henry asked.

"No, nothing." Eliza tapped her fingers on the table. "Why carry this around in her purse?"

Connie sat back in her chair. "Maybe there was bad blood when she left Mr Watson, but with them both being widowed she wanted to make amends."

"It's possible, but would she really need his address? I imagine that anyone familiar with the village knows where Clifftop House is."

"She may have wanted to write to him rather than turn up unannounced." Henry took the paper from Eliza. "She may have written to the person at the second address, too."

Eliza sat up straight. "Yes, of course! If she wrote to both, before she arrived, she could have arranged visits with them. In fact, it may have been Mr Watson she hoped to meet when she went missing."

"I doubt she visited Mr Watson." Connie's face was stern. "He's already told us he didn't know she was in St Giles and that he wouldn't have recognised her even if he had seen her."

Eliza smoothed the tablecloth with her fingers. "People do sometimes lie, especially if telling the truth would get them into trouble."

Henry handed back the paper. "We need to pay Mr Watson a visit, and this other person, to find out what they know. Shall we go now?"

Eliza nodded. "We can certainly call on Mr Watson."

Connie grabbed Eliza's hand. "Shouldn't we check with Maggie and Mr Scott first that this is Mrs Scott's purse? We'd look rather foolish if it's not."

Eliza stared at it as she turned it over in her hands. "No, I think we can be fairly certain this is the purse we're looking for. Once we've had dessert, I think we should visit Mr Watson, always assuming he's left the bar. We're better talking to him on his own rather than with everyone else."

The sun was still warm as they left the inn, and Eliza and Connie opened their parasols before crossing the road and heading up the hill.

"I shan't miss this walk once we get home." Eliza paused for breath as they reached the top.

"It is getting easier, though." Connie overtook Eliza. "At least I think it is."

"Thank goodness for small mercies." Archie chuckled as he held open the gate to Clifftop House. "Now, let me do the talking." He walked on ahead to knock on the front door.

It took more than a minute for Mr Watson to open it and he stared at them with bleary eyes. "May I help?"

Archie tipped his hat. "Good afternoon. I wonder if we could ask you a few more questions about Mrs Scott's death."

"I've nothing else to say. I've already told you, I hadn't

seen the woman for over twenty years and not spoken to her for nearer fifty."

Eliza stepped forward, a smile fixed on her face. "Yes, we understand that, but we've found evidence to suggest that Mrs Scott may have wanted to contact you. May we come in? It might be preferable to talking here."

Mr Watson eyed the four of them. "Very well." He opened the door wide before leading them into a well-stocked kitchen with a table in front of a large Georgian window at the far end.

"What a splendid view." Connie took the seat that was offered.

"The best in the village." Mr Watson glanced out of the window towards the sea and the headland before turning to Archie. "What's this evidence then?"

Archie sat down in the chair next to Eliza and gave her a barely perceptible nod.

"If I can answer that, Mr Watson." Eliza took out her pencil and paper. "On the day Mrs Scott's body was discovered, we found her handbag on the path that runs behind this house. Unfortunately, the purse had been taken and there was little else of interest."

Mr Watson's lips tightened. "As I said, I never use that path..."

"No, quite, but that's not why we're here." Eliza reached for the purse. "The thing is, we found it this morning in the churchyard, and it contained something rather interesting. A sheet of paper with two addresses on ... one of which was yours. We were wondering if you knew why Mrs Scott would have that with her."

"How would I know?" Mr Watson shrugged before he ran

a hand over his head. "We've had no contact with each other for nearly fifty years."

"So, she hadn't written to you?"

"Why would she do that?"

"That's what we can't fathom." Eliza tapped her pencil on the table.

"You'd be better off asking Mr Scott. If anyone had any idea of what was going on in her head, it's most likely to be him."

Eliza sat back in her chair as she studied Mr Watson. "Naturally, we'll speak with him, but we decided to come here first. We wondered if Mrs Scott was looking to rekindle your friendship."

Mr Watson snorted. "Not a chance. Her last words to me were that she never wanted to see me again."

Eliza wrinkled her nose. "Which makes it all the more confusing to find your address in her purse. Let me try a different tack. We know that you and Mrs Scott were once a couple. Can you tell us any more about your relationship ... or why she called it off? It might help."

Mr Watson studied Eliza before he sauntered to a cupboard near the door and poured himself a large Scotch. "There's not much to tell. We walked out together for about six months and I'd asked her to marry me."

"How long ago was this?"

"1856."

"So..." Eliza did the calculation in her head "...forty-six years ago."

"If you say so."

"If you were engaged to be married, what happened?"

Mr Watson took a large gulp of his Scotch. "You tell me.

143

Two months before the marriage ceremony she disappeared, and I heard nothing of her until I read in the newspaper that she'd married Mr Scott."

"How awful!" Connie put a hand to her mouth. "Didn't she give you an explanation?"

"Not a word."

"You must have been terribly angry with her."

Mr Watson sneered. "Why would you think that? Anyway, it was a long time ago, I'm over it."

"Did you confront her when you found out she was married?" Eliza asked.

"Not as such. Once she was wearing another man's wedding band, there was nothing I could do. I did bump into her once, shortly after she was married, and asked why she'd left, but that was when she said she hated me and never wanted to see me again. After that, I made it my business to stay out of her way."

"I imagine that was difficult in a village this size." Archie let out a low whistle.

For the first time, Mr Watson smiled. "Why do you think I fell into the habit of going to The Coach House? It was the one place I was confident she wouldn't visit."

"And you didn't see her again?" Eliza placed a hand on her chin.

"Not to talk to. If I ever saw her, I made a hasty retreat."

"So you don't know why she left St Giles?"

"Not got a clue, but I was mighty glad she did."

"Can I ask a question?" Henry had been sitting quietly beside his father. "Did you live here when you were walking out with Mrs Scott?"

"No, I was only young back then. I was in a fishermen's

144

cottage on the beach. That's why I'm so friendly with the men; I was once one of them."

"It's quite a jump to move from a small cottage to this." Eliza glanced around the large kitchen, with its extensive range of units.

"I worked hard and when I met the woman who became my wife, I didn't want her living down there."

"But you'd have lived there with Mrs Scott?"

"Not for long. We had talked about getting somewhere else, but obviously that didn't happen."

"Did you live in this house before Mrs Scott left the village, though?" Henry asked.

"Yes, I've been here years."

Henry looked to his mother. "So, she'd have known that, which takes us back to the original question. Why carry the address with her?"

Mr Watson walked to the door. "I'm sorry I can't help, but really, that woman was a law unto herself."

Eliza picked up her bag and stood up. "Actually, before we go, may I ask one more thing? The second address on the paper was for a house on Market Street in St Andrews. Might you know who lives there?"

Mr Watson smiled as he raised his glass. "Perhaps she was chasing another man."

Eliza chuckled. "The way this investigation's going, nothing would surprise me."

CHAPTER SIXTEEN

The sun was shining directly at the front door as Mr Watson showed his guests out and Eliza blinked several times to adjust her eyes to the light.

"I'm not sure we're any further advanced," she said as Archie closed the gate behind her.

"It was interesting about Mrs Scott leaving him as she did." Connie opened her parasol as they headed back to the village. "It's strange that he has no idea why she left."

"I imagine he was furious at the time." Archie pulled Eliza's hand through his arm. "I know I would have been."

"Your ma wouldn't have been so upset, though." Eliza gave him a sideways glance.

"She's getting used to it. I told her the other day I'd have stayed in London even if I hadn't met you."

Eliza chuckled. "Really? I bet she didn't like that."

"She huffed and puffed a bit, but if I can get her to stop blaming you for me being away, I'll be happy."

Eliza patted Archie's hand. "Thank you."

"Where are we going now?" Connie asked as they walked

past the shop.

"I thought we could visit Maggie to check the purse really is Mrs Scott's and ask if she knows anything about the addresses."

"I'm seeing Rabbie and Callum before they leave," Henry said. "We'll probably end up in The Coach House at some point."

"What are you going to do when they've gone?" Archie asked.

Henry shrugged. "Spend more time with you, I suppose." He glanced at his pocket watch. "I'd better get a move on; I'm late. See you later."

Archie watched him hurry down the hill. "I'm glad he's got on so well with everyone. Perhaps one day we can visit Fraser in Glasgow. It's easier to get there than here and I've not seen as much of him as I would have liked."

"I thought he'd been at your ma and pa's house while you were there."

"Oh, he has, but we don't have a chance to talk when Ma's around."

"Why not ask him to the inn tonight for a drink, just the two of you? I'm sure Connie and I can manage on our own."

Connie's eyes twinkled. "Of course we can; that's why you brought me, isn't it?"

"You know, I think I will." With a skip in his step, Archie increased the pace until they reached his sister's house. The front door was open, and Archie stepped to one side as he ushered Eliza and Connie past him. Maggie was stirring a pot on the range.

"My, that smells good." Eliza inhaled as she stepped into the kitchen. "May we come in?"

Maggie's smile was weak. "Of course, take a seat and I'll be with you in a minute. This broth's done now." She moved the broth from the heat and joined them at the table. "Have you any news?"

Eliza took Mrs Scott's purse from her handbag. "Do you recognise this?"

"Yes, of course. It's Ma's purse. Where did you find it?"

"Henry found it in the churchyard."

"Was there anything in it?" Maggie opened the clasp and took out the selection of papers.

"There was, but not there. We found this." She handed Maggie the paper with the addresses on it. "Do they make any sense to you?"

Maggie scratched the side of her head as she studied the note. "Well, it's her handwriting, but why would she have this?"

Archie shrugged. "That's what we can't figure out. We've spoken to Mr Watson, but he can't explain why his address was in the purse either."

"I don't suppose he could." She looked back at the paper. "Who lives on Market Street? Have you any thoughts?"

"No, none. We were hoping you or Mr Scott might know."

The corners of Maggie's mouth turned downwards. "I don't, and I doubt Robert will either. I'll ask him when he gets in."

"He's out?" Eliza's shoulders sagged. "Do you know when he'll be back?"

"Another hour or so. He's gone back to work."

"Of course. I'd forgotten it's Monday."

"You can wait if you like," Maggie said. "I'm only peeling

a few potatoes."

Archie shook his head. "We need to get back. Could you speak to Robert and find out if he has any ideas about the addresses?"

"I can ask..."

Eliza stood up but paused by the table. "Actually, while we're here, have the police been to see you?"

"The police?" The colour drained from Maggie's face. "No, why?"

Eliza patted her hand. "Don't look so worried. It's just that they called at Miss McGovern's this morning and have finally accepted that Mrs Scott was murdered. They've started making enquiries and so I imagine they'll want to speak to you. If it helps, I did point out that all the evidence suggests the murderer was a man."

Maggie visibly exhaled. "Oh, thank you. Do you think they believed you?"

"It's difficult to tell, but I'd suggest that if they come calling, you stay calm. It may be to your benefit."

Maggie nodded. "I'll try, thank you for the warning."

"Shall we go then?" Archie held open the door. "I need to get to Jean's before it's too late."

Once they were outside, Eliza slipped her arm through Archie's. "I've been thinking. Connie and I could go to Market Street tomorrow. We need to find out who lives there."

Archie stopped, his face stern. "You're not going to a strange house alone. You don't know who you'll find there."

"But that's why we need to go."

"No! It's not safe, two women travelling alone to find ... goodness knows what."

"Well, come with us."

Archie clicked his tongue as he carried on walking. "I've promised Fraser that I'll take him and the boys to the railway station. There won't be enough room in the carriage for all of us."

"But we're doing it for Maggie..."

After a long pause, Archie nodded. "Very well, but you must take Henry with you. Do you hear?"

Eliza's face broke into a smile. "I'm sure we can manage that and Henry won't mind."

They crossed over the road and walked along the edge of the beach towards Jean and Mr Stewart's house.

"There's no sign of Niall and Ross mending their nets. They mustn't have had as big a catch today."

Archie chuckled. "In that case, they'll probably be at The Coach House already. It's a hard life on the seas; they make the most of their time off."

"I suppose so. I hope Henry isn't picking up any bad habits from them."

"What like?"

"Like drinking too much. He's not used to it."

Archie gave her a sideways glance before stopping by the Stewarts' front doorstep. "I wouldn't be so sure; he goes to enough parties. Now, are you coming in?"

"We better had; we've not seen Jean as much as we have Maggie." Eliza took a deep breath as she reached for her handkerchief. "I can't imagine why."

Jean was chopping vegetables at the kitchen table as they went in.

"Are you on your own?" Archie asked.

"Everyone's at The Coach House; Fraser was hoping

you'd be there."

Archie rolled his eyes. "And here's me coming to invite him over tonight. Never mind, if he's there already, I'm sure I'll find him."

Jean pointed her knife at him. "Well, don't make him late for his tea. It'll be ready within the hour."

"As if I would ... as long as he's allowed out again later."

"Less of your cheek, Archie Thomson. Don't forget you're still my little brother."

Eliza chuckled. "You keep reminding him. It's a shame you can't join us; is Mr Stewart there?"

Jean glanced at the clock. "He may be by now, although he could still be at Clifftop House."

Eliza's eyebrows drew together. "Why would he be at Clifftop House?"

"He does a few odd jobs up there for Mr Watson; didn't he tell you?"

"No, he didn't."

"I'm surprised he finds the time," Archie said.

"Oh, he makes time." Jean's voice rang out around the kitchen. "Him and Mr Watson are as thick as thieves ... besides he makes it worth his while."

"What do you mean?"

"Mr Watson sees himself as quite the gentleman and doesn't care to do any manual work. He's always had someone go up there a few afternoons a week to do things like chopping logs, tidying the garden, that sort of thing."

"And Mr Stewart does that?"

"He does now. His father did it before him until his back started playing up."

"So what does Mr Watson provide in return?" Archie

raised an eyebrow.

"He keeps the rent low. He knows we're good tenants and so if we help him, he helps us."

"That sounds like a convenient arrangement." Archie winked at his sister.

"Oh, it is. It's saved us a lot of money over the years."

Eliza's forehead furrowed. "He must charge the other tenants more in rent then."

Jean wiped her hands on her apron and filled a pan with water. "Why do you say that?"

"He said he lived in one of the cottages on the beach before he moved up to Clifftop House so he must have got the money from somewhere."

Jean shrugged. "I suppose so; I've never really thought about it. He does have other business interests, though, not just the rents. He did a lot of errands for the church when Reverend Campbell was alive, and he still goes into St Andrews several times a week to do whatever it is he does."

"If Mr Stewart knows him well, could you find anything out from him?"

Jean grimaced. "I doubt it. You know what men are like, they don't talk about anything important. Besides, Mr Watson keeps himself to himself."

"Well, if you do find anything out, will you tell us? We don't want Maggie wrongly accused."

Jean banged her hand on the table. "No, we don't."

Archie picked up the hat he'd placed on the table. "Right, if we're done, we'd better be going. I want to catch Fraser before he leaves to come back here."

"And mind what I said," Jean called after them. "Don't keep them there too long."

CHAPTER SEVENTEEN

The noise from the bar spilled out onto the street as Archie held open the door of The Coach House.

"Gosh, it sounds busy in there." Connie hesitated before going in.

"It does, it's really no place for ladies. Let me take a quick look in the bar to see if Fraser's there and then I'll order a drink for you in the dining room. You'll be fine in there."

Eliza waited in the hall, but once Archie disappeared, she followed him to the door and peered into the bar.

Connie crept up behind her. "What's going on?"

"Archie's found Fraser with Henry and the boys, they're in the back corner where we usually sit, but Jean was right about Mr Watson and Mr Stewart. They're on their own at a table by the front window with their heads together."

"Is there anyone else in there?"

"The fishermen we saw the other day are by the bar." Eliza chuckled. "They already look as if they've had a drink too many."

"I wonder if we could talk to them," Connie said. "They might be a little more talkative."

Eliza withdrew back into the hall. "That's an excellent idea. How do we do it, though? We can't just go in; Archie would be beside himself."

Connie chewed down on her lip. "Would he notice if we sneaked in?"

Eliza peered into the bar again. "I imagine so. Confound it, Henry's seen us and he's coming over."

"Maybe he could help."

"What are you two doing? You're acting very suspiciously."

"Shh." Eliza checked on Archie before pulling Henry into the hall. "Did your father notice you leave?"

"I doubt it, he's too busy talking to Uncle Fraser. What do you want?"

"We'd like to speak to Mr Burns and the fishermen we spoke to the other day, but we don't want Mr Watson or your father to know."

"Ah." Henry gave them a knowing wink. "Leave it to me. You go into the dining room and wait for them there."

"What will you say?"

Henry gave Eliza a lopsided grin. "I've not decided yet."

Once Henry disappeared Eliza and Connie crossed the hallway.

"Do you know what you'll ask them?" Connie asked.

"Not yet, but I'm wondering if they could shed more light on Mrs Scott's past. I'm sure it's got something to do with this whole affair. If we could find out a bit more about it from them..."

A frown crossed Connie's face. "Hasn't Mr Watson told us already?"

"He's told us his version of events, but people see things differently. Why don't we find out what they've got to say."

They only waited a minute before Mr Burns led Mr McKay, Mr Cargill and Mr Dowie in to join them.

"The young man said you wanted to talk to us." Mr Burns took a seat at the table next to theirs and indicated for his friends to join him.

"We did. Thank you for coming." Eliza stood up to close the door. "We're still wondering about Mrs Scott's death and can't help thinking her early years in St Giles may help explain it. Can you tell us what she was like all those years ago?"

The men stared at each other. "What sort of things are you interested in?"

"Well, for example, Mr Watson's told us about his engagement to..." Eliza scanned her notes "...to Miss Davison as she was then, and how she left him and married Mr Scott. Do you remember anything about that? How upset or angry was he?"

"We're not going to be telling no tales." Mr Dowie banged his glass on the table. "He's one of us, Mr Watson is."

"Oh, quite, and I wouldn't expect you to tell tales. He told us how he used to live on the beach beside you when he was walking out with Miss Davison."

"Aye, the one next door to me," Mr Cargill said.

"So it must have come as a surprise when he bought Clifftop House."

"Why would it?" Mr Burns took a sip of his ale. "He'd had his eye on it for years and he worked hard for it."

"I'm sure he did, but ... well, the thing that's puzzling me is that you must work hard too, and yet ... well ... you're still there."

"He always had his eyes on bigger things, not that he ever told us what he was up to," Mr McKay said. "He just gets on with it and fits back in with the rest of us when he's ready."

"I blame that woman."

Eliza looked over to Mr Dowie. "You mean Mrs Watson?"

"No, not her, although she benefitted from it. I mean Miss Davison. They were due to be married, but she refused to live in the cottage, told him he had to find somewhere better for her ... so he did."

Eliza's brow creased. "So, he bought Clifftop House for her, but she left him, anyway?"

"Not exactly." Mr Dowie's words were slurring. "They went to view it and he said he'd buy it for her, but before all the legal stuff happened, she'd gone."

"So, she knew he was buying the house?"

"And had even been to see it," Connie added.

"And yet she still wasn't happy. He was lucky to be shut of her..." Mr Dowie's voice grew louder.

"That's very interesting." Eliza paused. "Tell me, did Mr Scott have a bigger or better house than Mr Watson? Might that be why she left?"

Again, the men looked at each other before Mr Burns answered. "Not at all. If you must know, he lived in a cottage not much bigger than the ones on the beach."

"So, she wouldn't marry Mr Watson despite his promise to buy her the house she wanted, and yet she did marry Mr Scott and moved into his smaller house."

"She married Mr Scott rather quickly too, didn't she?" Connie said.

Mr Cargill let out a low whistle. "I'd say she did. Within a couple of months if I remember rightly."

"Had she known him prior to leaving Mr Watson?"

"Och, aye. She was quite a one for the men in those days. If I'm honest, there weren't many of us who'd have turned her down, but she knew it. Mr Scott was just that much keener than the rest of us. He'd admired her for years but until she left Mr Watson, she'd never given him a second glance."

Eliza looked to Connie. "So it was unlikely she left Mr Watson because she'd suddenly been swept off her feet."

Mr McKay laughed. "That certainly wasn't the case. Mr Scott was as surprised as the rest of us when they got together."

"That's right." Mr Dowie waved his glass at Eliza. "To start with Mr Scott wondered if Mr Watson had mistreated her, which was why she was in such a hurry to get away, but that was only his imagination. Mrs Scott, as she was by then, never said a word and we all knew Mr Watson wouldn't do such a thing. Once the dust had settled, it wasn't mentioned again."

"Did Mr Watson ever confront her?"

Mr Burns shook his head. "There was no point. He was certainly angry that she'd made a fool of him, but he had too much dignity to face her or Mr Scott. Not when there wasn't anything he could do about it. No, he just found himself another wife, completed the purchase of Clifftop House and made sure everyone knew he and his wife were happy together."

"And were they?"

"Aye, I'd say they were. For the most part."

"I'd say he was much happier than he would have been with Mrs Scott," Mr Dowie said. "She turned into a right miserable woman once Robert was born, not that anyone had any sympathy for her."

"But they were happy before then?"

"To be honest, nobody paid much attention," Mr Burns said. "In the end, it was Mr Scott everyone felt sorry for."

Eliza scribbled a note onto her paper. "We've been told that their son, Robert, didn't get on with his father. Do you think that could be why Mr and Mrs Scott argued?"

"I'm sure they argued about him, but that wasn't all." Mr McKay glanced around at his friends. "Do you remember, they'd argue about anything and everything? I even heard Mr Scott said he was sorry he married her."

There were nods around the table.

Connie's eyebrows drew together. "So, if they disliked each other so much, why did they move away to the middle of nowhere to rear sheep?"

All the men shrugged.

"You won't get an answer to that, not now they're both dead." Mr Burns paused for confirmation. "There was a rumour it was because Mrs Scott didn't like her new daughter-in-law, but I can't say how much truth there was to that."

Eliza put the end of her pencil to her lips. "I'll grant you there wasn't any love lost between the two Mrs Scotts, but could the murder have been because of something that happened in St Giles before the Scotts left? Something that reared its head again once she decided to move back?"

Mr Burns stood up to leave. "Well, it was nothing to do with any of us ... or Mr Watson for that matter. We've known each other long enough for me to say that with confidence. I'd suggest you speak to Maggie Scott again. As I understand it, she was the last person to see her alive. Now, if you'll excuse me." He waved an empty tankard in the air.

"One moment." Eliza flicked back through her notepaper. "Who told you that?"

Mr Burns flicked his eyes around the room. "You did."

Eliza shook her head. "I don't think so."

Mr Burns shrugged. "It must have been the police then."

"The police!" Eliza was on her feet. "Have you seen them?"

"They came into the bar this lunchtime and spoke to all of us."

Eliza's stomach sank. "What did they want?"

"Much the same as you, but they seemed very interested in Maggie Scott. They asked when we'd last seen her."

"And the last time you saw her was when she walked past you with old Mrs Scott?"

"Correct." Mr Burns turned to leave, causing the others to follow.

"I don't like the sound of that." Eliza flopped back down onto her seat as the men left. "Have they really not got beyond that?"

"Have we?" Connie asked. "Our stranger's turned out not to be so strange, the men in the village can all give each other alibis for the afternoon in question and the bend in the road stopped Miss McGovern from seeing anything important. You must admit, given the relationship between the two Mrs Scotts, it doesn't look good."

Eliza ran her hands across her face. "You're right, it doesn't, but we can't let the police arrest Maggie. Let's hope the house in St Andrews has some relevance to all this. Maggie wouldn't have gone there. Not on her own."

CHAPTER EIGHTEEN

The following morning Connie knocked on Eliza's bedroom door and the two of them made their way downstairs.

"We may be early, but where is everyone?" Connie glanced around the empty dining room. "Where's Dr Thomson this morning? And Henry?"

Eliza rolled her eyes. "I don't know about Henry, but Archie's in no fit state to join us. It's as well he doesn't see his brother more often given the amount of whisky they must have drunk last night."

Connie gasped and put a hand to her mouth. "Isn't he taking his brother and the boys to the railway station this morning?"

"If Fraser's anything like Archie, he won't be in any hurry to sit on a train. He'll have to take the one this afternoon."

"But what about our trip to St Andrews? Henry's supposed to be chaperoning us."

A mischievous grin crossed Eliza's face. "We'll just have to take the carriage ourselves."

"We can't do that … can we?" Connie's eyes were wide. "What will Dr Thomson say?"

Eliza flicked her napkin onto her lap. "Right now, he's in no position to say anything and if he doesn't want his sister arrested for murder, he'd better give us his blessing."

"Yes, of course, but it doesn't seem right."

A waitress put a pot of tea in the middle of the table. "Will you be wanting kippers this morning, ladies?"

Eliza shook her head. "No, thank you. A couple of slices of toast will be fine, we're in a hurry."

With their tea and toast finished, Eliza picked up her handbag and was about to leave when Henry joined them. The paleness of his skin highlighted the dark shadows under his eyes.

"I take it you had a good time last night." Eliza pulled out a chair for him as she stood up. "I'm afraid you'll have to have breakfast on your own, unless you've heard from your father."

"Where are you going?"

"To the address in St Andrews; I told you yesterday."

"But you can't go without me!"

Eliza grinned at Connie. "You should have thought about that last night. Besides, I have a job for you here that'll be a better use of your time."

Henry's shoulders slumped. "What sort of job?"

"I want you to go to the church and ask the reverend if you can search through the parish register. I'm interested in anything you can find about Mrs Scott. Start in the year 1856 and find out when she was married, whether it was by special licence, when Robert was baptised and anything else that may be of interest."

Connie's eyebrows drew together. "What are you looking for?"

"I'm not certain, but I'm hoping we can uncover something that starts to make some sense of all this." She looked back to Henry. "In fact, start a year earlier than that. Double- check she hadn't already married Mr Watson before she left him."

"She couldn't have done that..." Connie's mouth dropped open.

Eliza sighed. "No, you're probably right ... but have a look, anyway. Now, Connie, I've arranged for a carriage to pick us up in five minutes. Henry, we'll meet you back here for luncheon."

With the sun shining on them from over the sea, the ride into St Andrews was pleasant, despite a number of ruts in the road that caused the carriage to rock, sometimes violently, from side to side.

"At least it's not far." Eliza clung onto a strap near the window.

"I don't remember it being this bumpy on the way here."

"That's because we had Archie and Henry with us, not to mention all our luggage to weigh us down. I suppose there's something to be said for having a man to chaperone you."

Connie laughed. "Well, I hope it's worth the journey. I'd hate to get there and find the house empty."

"I hadn't thought of that." Eliza put a hand on Connie's arm. "Blimey, I've had a thought. What if Mrs Scott had this address because this is where she was moving to?"

"Why would she move here when Maggie and Mr Scott are in St Giles? From everything I've heard, I would say she'd deliberately move to St Giles, possibly even to their house, just to upset them."

Eliza nodded. "You're right; I suppose we'll find out when we get there."

Ten minutes later, the carriage pulled up outside the centre of a row of small terraced houses.

"They're not very smart," Connie said. "I thought everywhere around here would be nice."

"I expect you get places like this everywhere." Eliza accepted the driver's assistance as she climbed down from the carriage.

"Shall we ask the coachman to wait?" Connie asked. "I'd feel safer if he did."

"Yes, that's a good idea. It will help calm Archie down later, too." Eliza turned to the man who stood waiting for his fee. "Sir, would you mind knocking on the door for us and then waiting? We don't know who'll answer or how long we'll be."

With a nod, the coachman rapped on the door-knocker before stepping back, leaving Eliza and Connie to wait. Seconds later the door was opened by a man Eliza felt she already knew.

"Mr Carmichael?"

The man's dark brown eyes flicked between them as Eliza studied his overly big jacket and greying hair. It had to be him.

"Yes?"

"May we have a word with you? I'm Mrs Thomson and this is my companion, Mrs Appleton."

"I-I suppose so. Would you like to come in?"

Eliza hesitated and glanced at Connie before looking both ways up the street.

"Perhaps we can stay here. It seems quiet enough."

The man nodded. "As you wish ... how may I help?"

"We'd like to ask if you're acquainted with a lady called Mrs Scott."

The man's face remained blank. "I don't think so. Should I be?"

"We can't be certain, but if I describe her, you may recognise her. She's rather elderly, but attractive with pale grey hair and blue eyes."

"And quite slim," Connie added.

"I-I may have seen her. Why?" His eyes continued to flick between them as he clenched his hands before him.

"Mrs Scott was part of my husband's family and I'm sorry to say she was found dead last week."

"F-found d-dead?"

"I'm afraid so. We're hoping to make some sense of it and one of the things we found in her handbag was a piece of paper with this address written on."

The colour drained from Mr Carmichael's face. "Is that how you knew my name?"

"No, not exactly. You were seen in St Giles last week and so I took the liberty of asking after you. Reverend Rennie recognised your description."

A weak smile crossed his lips. "He's a nice man, the minister."

Eliza nodded. "He is. We didn't know you lived here, but we wanted to find out who did and ask if you had any idea why Mrs Scott would be carrying around your address."

"I-I don't know. I'd never met her before ... but she wrote to me..."

"She wrote to you?" A spark of excitement raced down Eliza's spine. "When was that?"

"About ten days ago, but she didn't give her name."

"Would you mind telling us what she wanted?"

"She asked me to meet her in St Giles because she had something to tell me."

Eliza nodded. "That's interesting. Did she give any hint of what it was about?"

Mr Carmichael paused for such a long time Eliza wondered if he'd lost his tongue.

"Mr Carmichael? Could you give us an idea?"

"She said ... she said it was about my parents."

Eliza's forehead creased. "Forgive me for the intrusion, but when I spoke to Reverend Rennie about you, he told me your parents were dead."

The man nodded. "They are, or at least I thought they were; I wrote back and said as much."

"Did she reply?"

"No." Mr Carmichael wiped a hand across his forehead. "She came to visit me."

Eliza and Connie were both open-mouthed as they turned to each other.

"She came here?" Eliza struggled to get her words out. "When?"

"Late on Thursday morning. I live on my own and I was getting myself something to eat."

Connie touched Eliza on the arm. "That would have been when Mr Scott picked her up from Cupar."

"It would." Eliza held Mr Carmichael's gaze. "Did she have a man with her when she called? Someone of a similar age to you, with dark hair?"

Mr Carmichael shook his head. "No, she was alone."

"And did she tell you anything about your parents?"

Mr Carmichael looked up and down the street. "This is no place to discuss it; if you won't come in, perhaps we could walk to the park. I'd rather not be overheard."

Eliza glanced round, but seeing no signs of anything green, she walked over to the coachman. A moment later she returned. "We're welcome to sit in the carriage, if that suits you."

With a nod, Mr Carmichael pulled the door closed behind him and followed the ladies to the carriage. Once he was settled on the seat facing them, Eliza tried again.

"So, what was it she wanted to tell you?"

"I didn't find out. She was very evasive, insisting I go to St Giles that afternoon to hear the truth."

"The truth about your parents?"

Mr Carmichael studied his hands as they rested on his knees. "The thing is, I haven't had a good life. I was born around here somewhere, but my parents only kept me for a year before they sent me to an orphanage in Edinburgh. It was years later when I found out it was because they didn't have the money to feed themselves, let alone me, and so they must have thought that sending me away was for the best."

"Did they tell you that?'

Mr Carmichael shook his head but continued to stare at his hands. "No. Life in the orphanage was miserable but at least I had a roof over my head, but then everything changed when I reached sixteen. I was too old to stay and was basically put out on the streets. The matron told me before I left that I'd arrived from St Andrews and so I came back here to try and find my family."

Eliza's tone was soft. "And did you?"

"No. They were already dead. My father had apparently drunk himself into an early grave and my mother ... well, she didn't remarry and died alone. According to the minister, they had no more children."

"So, what did you do?" Connie's voice cracked as she spoke.

"I was fortunate. I managed to get work on the fishing boats, which gives me enough money to pay the rent here."

"So news of your parents would have been irrelevant. You never really knew them."

Mr Carmichael clasped his fingers together. "That's what I thought when I got the letter, but things changed when she came to see me." He looked up at Eliza. "The thing is, she told me that the couple I'd thought of as my family had actually only adopted me, and that I had a ma and pa who were still alive ... and living in St Giles."

Connie gasped. "And you knew nothing of this?"

Mr Carmichael once again bowed his head. "Nothing at all." He ran his fingers across his eyes. "For all these years I'd assumed my parents hadn't wanted me, but now it seems that there were two couples who gave me away."

"You can't think that." Eliza suppressed her urge to reach out for his hand. "There are many reasons you could have been with Mr and Mrs Carmichael. Did Mrs Scott give you any more information when she visited?"

"No, but she hinted that they lived on St Andrews Road and that she'd introduce me if I met her on the headland."

"So that explains why you were in the village on Thursday."

He nodded. "She told me there was a bench, and that I

was to meet her there at quarter past two. I was a few minutes early so when she wasn't there I waited by the church, but she didn't turn up."

"Did you see anyone while you were there?"

"A couple of people. One of them was a man who seemed to be watching me from the house opposite. As soon as I saw him, I disappeared into the churchyard. I know what small villages can be like with strangers."

Eliza groaned. "Yes, we all do. Could you describe him?"

Mr Carmichael paused as he stared out of the window. "Not really, he was a fair distance away. He was an older man and looked reasonably smart. Grey hair, I think."

Eliza nodded. *Mr Watson.*

"Who else?"

"There was a woman with red hair. She arrived not long after I'd gone into the churchyard. She came out of the shop and seemed to be in quite a panic when she reached the bench. She disappeared towards St Andrews but was back about twenty minutes later ... looking even more distraught."

"What did she do then?"

"She headed down the hill into St Giles."

Maggie's alibi. Eliza gave him a subdued smile. "Was there anyone else?"

"Not on the headland, not that I saw, anyway."

"How long did you stay?"

Mr Carmichael hesitated. "I waited until the church bell struck three o'clock."

"And then you made your way back to St Andrews?"

"I walked. Because Mrs Scott had hinted that my real parents lived on St Andrews Road, I stopped to look at the houses. They're a lot smarter than the ones around here." He stared through the window once more. "There was one house where a woman caught me staring, and so after that, I got a move on and came straight home."

Miss McGovern. Eliza gave an inward sigh of relief. "That's very helpful, thank you for being so honest. There's one more thing. Why did you go back to St Giles on Friday?"

This time there was no hesitation, only sadness. "Curiosity, I suppose. I still hoped that Mrs Scott would turn up."

So he'd no idea of the murder?

"Did she say anything to suggest who your parents might be? If she did, we may be able to help identify them."

Mr Carmichael sighed. "No, that's the thing, she wouldn't give me any clue as to who my father was, only that I'd find out where he lived if I did as she asked." He looked up and held Eliza's gaze. "I tried my best to do what she wanted, but she disappeared. I just don't know what to do now."

Eliza reached out and took his hand. He flinched as he felt her fingers, but she kept her hand where it was. "Am I right in thinking that you hadn't heard about Mrs Scott's *accident*?"

"Accident?"

"I'm afraid that when her body was found on Friday morning, we had reason to believe she'd been murdered."

"Murdered!" His eyes became wild. "Is that why you're here, because you think I had something to do with it?"

"No, no, please don't think that." Eliza let go of his hand as he reached for the carriage door. "We came because your address was in Mrs Scott's handbag and we didn't know why. Now you've explained it, well ... perhaps you could help us identify the killer."

"No, I've told you all I can. There was the smartly dressed

man, and a woman with red hair. I didn't see anyone else on the street. Please, you have to let me go. I wish I'd never met the woman."

He jumped from the carriage before bolting back to the house, slamming the door behind him.

"Well." Eliza sank back on the seat.

"Well, indeed." Connie leaned against the side of the carriage. "What do we do now?"

Eliza remained silent, thoughts racing through her head until she finally sat up straight. "The first thing we need to do is speak to Mr Scott and confirm that he brought his mother here on Thursday morning. If he did, then I'd say there's a good chance Maggie has her alibi."

"Yes, of course. Mr Carmichael saw her doing what she said she'd done."

"But first we must eat." Eliza let out a sigh. "I need a fresh pot of tea and time to think about this. Driver, will you take us back to St Giles, please."

There was no sign of Henry when they returned to the inn, but Archie was at the dining table reading the newspaper.

"Ah, here you are." Eliza found the most cheerful voice she could muster. "How's your head?"

"It's fine, thank you, but stop trying to distract me. Where've you been?"

"I told you we were going to St Andrews, to the address Mrs Scott had in her purse."

"Where's Henry?"

Eliza glanced around the room. "I couldn't say for certain. He really wasn't well this morning and so I asked him to do some checking for me at church. He's been an awfully long time if he's still there."

Archie's face stiffened. "I told you not to go to St Andrews on your own. It's not safe. And before you say anything, going with Mrs Appleton does not count as having a chaperone."

"Oh, don't be such a worrier. The coachman stayed with us."

Archie banged his hand on the table. "A coachman you'd never met before. For all you know, he could be the killer."

"Now you're being ridiculous." Eliza took a seat opposite her husband. "We were perfectly safe, weren't we, Connie?"

"Don't bring me into it." Connie's cheeks coloured as Archie stared at her.

"I'm not bringing you into it, I just want Archie to realise that he's being overprotective." She put her arms on the table and leaned forward to gaze into his eyes. "Don't you want to know what we found out?"

Archie's lips twitched as he struggled to keep his face straight. "Not particularly."

Eliza threw her head back with a laugh. "Of course you do, you just don't want to admit it. Well, to save you asking, we've found our stranger and he can provide an alibi for Maggie."

Archie looked to Connie for confirmation.

"It's true."

"All right then." He sat back and folded his arms. "I'm listening."

CHAPTER NINETEEN

With lunch over and the teapot empty, Archie walked around the table to help Eliza and Connie from their seats.

"Right, let's go and see what Mr Scott has to say, shall we?" Eliza stepped around the table.

"Aren't you going to wait for me?"

She flinched as Henry hurried into the dining room.

"What have you been doing? I was beginning to think you'd got lost."

Henry's face was rather sheepish. "It's so dark in the church and with one thing and another..."

Eliza rolled her eyes. "You fell asleep, didn't you?"

"It wasn't for long, but you've seen what it's like in there."

"Well, for that you'll have to eat on your own and follow us to your aunty and uncle's house later." She indicated to Connie to start walking. "Oh, assuming you were awake long enough to look through the register, did you find anything of interest about Mrs Scott?"

"No, nothing out of the ordinary." The twinkle returned to his eyes. "I did find out some gossip, though."

Eliza picked up her handbag. "I'm afraid it will have to wait. We need to visit Mr Scott while he's home for lunch; we can catch up on gossip tonight."

Eliza stared up at the sky as she stepped outside The Coach House and waited for Connie and Archie.

Connie shivered as she joined her. "It's cool when the sun goes behind the clouds."

"I'm afraid it's one of the perils of being on the east coast of Scotland." Archie offered Eliza his arm. "Summer arrives late and leaves early. In another month, you'll need a thick coat."

"It's nice while it lasts, though." Connie strolled alongside Eliza, using her parasol as a walking stick. "It's a shame we haven't had more time to explore the place."

"Which means the sooner we find our murderer the better. We still have a few days." She turned to Archie. "I forgot to ask you, did Fraser get away this morning?"

"He did. He called at the inn while I was having breakfast and said they'd arranged a carriage to take them to the railway station."

"And was he in as bad a state as you?" Eliza kept her face straight.

"He's more used to it than I am." Archie nodded towards Maggie's house as it came into view. "It looks like they've got visitors."

Eliza studied the chestnut horses that stood in front of an elaborate wooden-framed carriage. "Whoever it is could be visiting one of the neighbours."

"It's rather splendid, though, a lot smarter than the one we travel..." Connie stopped as Eliza nudged her in the ribs.

Shush. Eliza mouthed the words. *Don't remind him.*

Connie's lips twisted. "Sorry."

Archie appeared too focussed on the carriage to notice. "Who'd be visiting anyone around here in a carriage like that?"

Eliza kept her voice light. "Shall we go and find out?"

After examining the workmanship of the carriage at close quarters, Archie ushered the ladies to the Scotts' front door. "Maggie, are you in?"

Maggie hurried to the door and without a word of explanation pushed them straight into the kitchen.

"What's going on?" Archie turned around as she shut the door behind them.

"Ma's solicitor's here from Edinburgh."

"Ah, so that explains the carriage." Archie placed his hat on the table. "I didn't think it belonged to anyone from around here. Has he brought the will?"

"No, nothing like that. He's the solicitor who's selling her house in Cupar; he hadn't heard about her death. He wanted her to sign some papers." Maggie glanced back at the door. "But that's not all."

Butterflies fluttered in Eliza's stomach. "What else is there?"

Maggie sat at the table, her hands clasped before her. "He's come to discuss her move to Clifftop House."

"Clifftop House!" Eliza spun around to Archie. "How could that be? Mr Watson swore he'd had no contact with her."

Archie raised an eyebrow. "Maybe he hadn't. If she'd

175

instructed a solicitor, all correspondence could have been through him. He needn't have seen her."

"The crafty devil. It didn't even cross my mind, although you'd still have thought he'd have mentioned it."

"It would explain why Mrs Scott had the address in her purse," Connie said. "She would have needed it for the solicitor."

"You're right." Maggie nodded to herself.

"What do you mean?" Eliza studied her sister-in-law.

"Apparently, Ma told the solicitor she wanted Clifftop House and had given him the details, but she told him she'd speak to the current owner when she got here."

"So, you reckon she was planning to do that on Thursday afternoon when you walked her to the shop? Meet with Mr Watson."

"I think it was, although whether she actually saw him is another matter."

"We've spoken to him a couple of times and he's adamant he hasn't seen her for twenty years."

"Perhaps she called at the house, but he wasn't in," Connie said.

"It's certainly possible." Eliza bit down on her bottom lip. "We'll need to call on him again and find out what he knows. Has the solicitor said anything about why she wanted to move back?"

"She told him it was because she was a burden to Robert and hoped to make life easier for him."

"That's nice of her." A smile settled on Connie's lips.

Maggie shook her head. "It's a lie. She wouldn't do anything unless there was something in it for her. Trust me on that."

"Surely being closer to her family would have been enough?"

"You didn't know her. If we were so important, why did she move away in the first place?"

Eliza interrupted. "Have you been sitting in on the conversations with the solicitor?"

"After a fashion. I was in the room, but he was only interested in what Robert had to say."

"Did you hear him mention a Mr Carmichael who lives in St Andrews?"

Maggie let out a sigh. "We spent the first twenty minutes telling him about her death and we've not long since been talking about Clifftop House."

"Do you think we could ask him? Mr Scott, too. It's rather important."

Maggie chewed on her lip. "Wait here and I'll go and ask."

She hadn't been gone a minute before she came back and invited them into the living room. The solicitor was a large, rotund man with greying hair and a moustache. He glared at them through a monocle as they walked in.

"Thank you for seeing us, sir." Archie introduced them.

"Well, Dr Thomson, what may I do for you?" The solicitor straightened his back as he spoke.

"Actually, it's my wife who has some questions. Would you indulge her?"

With a loud harrumph, the solicitor turned to Eliza. "Yes?"

"We were wondering if Mrs Scott ever mentioned a Mr Donald Carmichael to you. He lives in St Andrews, but she had his address in her purse."

The solicitor's jowls wobbled as he shook his head. "I can't say she did. Is that it?"

Eliza's face flushed. "May I ask the same question of Mr Scott?"

"Me?" Mr Scott spun around to face Eliza. "Why would she have told me?"

Eliza pursed her lips. "Am I right in thinking that when you picked your mother up last Thursday, you didn't bring her straight here? Instead, you stopped off in St Andrews, which is what caused you to be late."

"You did what...?"

Eliza held up her hand to silence Maggie as Mr Scott fidgeted with his fingers. The eyes of those in the room stared at him. Eventually, he spoke. "Yes, we did stop, but I don't know why."

Eliza raised an eyebrow at him.

"Ma asked me to take her to the church there because she wanted to speak to someone. Once we got there, she told me to wait before she disappeared."

"You don't know where she went?"

"No, she took a right-hand turn and disappeared for about ten minutes. When she came back, she had a look of satisfaction on her face, but wouldn't say what she'd been doing."

"Is the church near Market Street by any chance?"

"Yes, that's the road she went down."

"But you've never heard of a man called Donald Carmichael?"

"No, never."

"Maggie, what about you?"

"No, why?"

"Because he was the man Mrs Scott visited when you took her to St Andrews. He's also the man people have described as being in St Giles on the afternoon of her death."

"So he's the killer?" Mr Scott's eyes were wide as Maggie broke into a broad grin.

"You've found him. Oh, Eliza, thank you."

Eliza held up her hands. "No, I'm sorry. You misunderstood me. We now know who Mr Carmichael is, but I don't believe he killed Mrs Scott."

"He didn't?" Maggie was crestfallen.

Eliza patted her sister-in-law's arm. "He may be able to help us, though. Just give me more time." Eliza turned her attention back to the solicitor. "I'm sorry to have taken up so much of your time, sir, but would you mind if I ask one more question? Had Mr Watson agreed to sell Clifftop House to Mrs Scott?"

"Not that I'm aware of. That's one of the reasons for my visit. I've written to him on three occasions but so far he's failed to respond."

"So he knew of Mrs Scott's intentions?" Eliza tapped her fingers on her chin. "That's very interesting. Thank you."

Maggie had just closed the front door after them when Henry appeared, running towards them.

"What's up with you?" Archie asked once he joined them.

Henry paused for breath. "The police are at the inn again."

Eliza took hold of his arm and started walking. "What do they want?"

"I'm not certain. If I'm being honest, they don't seem to have much idea of what they're doing."

Eliza increased her pace. "Have they said anything we haven't heard already?"

Henry shook his head. "Not so far, but I started to worry when they continued to focus on Aunty Maggie."

"What did they say?" Archie's tone was brusque as he kept step with his son.

"They just kept saying that she was the last person to see Mrs Scott alive and were trying to find the evidence to pin the blame on her."

Archie broke into a dash. "We'd better hurry."

The two women struggled to keep up, but Eliza held onto Henry's arm to slow him down. "Tell me..." she paused for breath "...did anyone say anything that could incriminate her?"

They were at the door to the inn when Henry answered. "Unfortunately, one of them did. Mr Stewart."

Eliza gasped and pushed past Henry as she hurried to the bar. Archie was already beside the sergeant.

"Good afternoon, Sergeant."

"Dr Thomson." Sergeant Mitchell stared at Archie before he noticed Eliza and Connie. "Mrs Thomson. This is most irregular having women in the bar."

"Forgive me, but as far as I'm aware, it's not illegal, and I'm interested to know how your investigation's progressing. I imagine you're much further on with things than we are."

The sergeant puffed out his chest. "It's going very well."

"Splendid." Eliza forced a smile to her lips. "So, are you close to arresting anyone?"

"We are as it happens. As with all murder cases, it's

usually the most obvious suspect that turns out to be the killer. There's no need to be clever."

"Oh, I'm sure there's no danger of you doing that; I just can't help looking for clues in places I needn't. Do you have any witnesses to what happened?"

"No, not exactly, but we've all agreed that Mrs Maggie Scott was the last person to see old Mrs Scott alive. Knowing how they disliked each other it makes sense to have her as the key suspect."

Eliza cocked her head to one side. "I'm sorry, I must be mistaken, I thought we'd decided it was more likely to be a man who committed the murder ... given the cause of death and the distance of the body from the headland."

"Ah yes, but as Mr Scott was about to lose his job, we all feel she most probably became hysterical and found an inner strength to cause the injuries." He indicated to the men around the bar, who all nodded in agreement.

"Who said he was about to lose his job?" Eliza eyed each man at the bar as the sergeant spoke.

"Well, no one in so many words, but with the amount of time he was spending in Cupar, you could see it coming. That would give Maggie Scott a strong motive."

Eliza put a hand to her head. "You can't suspect someone of murder based on something that hasn't happened. I've just left the Scotts' house and there's no indication he'll lose his job."

"They're hardly likely to own up to it, are they?" Mr Stewart spoke from the corner of the room where he shared a table with Mr Watson.

"What are you saying, man?" Archie's face was like

thunder. "The Scotts are part of the family and Maggie's my sister. She wouldn't do anything like that."

Mr Stewart shrugged. "I'm sorry, but if she's guilty..."

"But she isn't." Eliza turned to Archie, unable to hide her disbelief.

A snide grin crept across the sergeant's lips. "You know that for sure, do you?"

"Actually, I do." Eliza glared at him. "I've spoken to someone who saw her on the day in question doing exactly what she said she did."

"And who would that be?" Mr Stewart's eyes were like slits. "I don't believe it's anyone here."

"Someone who was walking along the headland."

The sergeant reached for his notebook. "We've spoken to everyone in the village and there was no one else on the headland at that time. I need the name and address of your witness."

Eliza felt the eyes of everyone in the bar staring at her. "I can't say."

"Ha. Because they don't exist." Mr Stewart took a deep swig of his ale.

"Mrs Thomson, may I remind you that it's an offence to withhold information from the police."

"I'm not withholding it, but I won't give the name of an innocent man to a room of inebriated men who are looking to blame an equally innocent woman."

"If they were on the headland at the right time, how do you know they're not the guilty party? They could have been an accomplice." Mr Stewart stepped forward and placed his empty tankard on the bar.

"Because I've spoken to him..."

"Is this the stranger some of us saw that afternoon?" Mr Watson pulled on the back of Mr Stewart's jacket. "Come and sit down."

Eliza nodded. "As soon as the police speak to him, they'll find out the truth."

"You mean you'd rather believe a stranger than the people who've welcomed you into the village?" Mr Burns didn't take his eyes from her until Eliza stepped towards Archie and took his arm.

"Gentlemen, please. There's no need to be hostile." Archie patted Eliza's hand. "This is a murder investigation and we need to arrest the right man. Sergeant Mitchell, could we have a word with you in private? My wife's discovered some information that could prove quite interesting."

"But, she's..."

"Yes, she's a woman, but she has experience in these matters. Please, humour me. If it makes you feel any better, I'll be with her."

"I'll join you, too." Henry stepped forward.

Eliza held up her hand. "No. Can you wait with Connie? We'll talk later."

CHAPTER TWENTY

Eliza tidied her notes on the dining table after she'd told the sergeant of her visit to St Andrews. He sat back in his seat studying her, unable to keep the smirk from his face.

"I'm sure that's very thorough of you, Mrs Thomson, but you're no closer to finding the killer than we are."

"Not yet, but we're getting nearer." Eliza hesitated and straightened the papers once more. "I believe the men in the bar are hiding something. Why else would they be so hostile when I'm trying to stop a woman from being wrongly accused?"

"You think one of them's the murderer?"

"I didn't say that, but I would say that if it isn't one of them, then they know who it is."

"I must agree with my wife," Archie said. "I can't deny I was shocked by Mr Stewart; he's my brother-in-law and yet he's blaming my sister."

"Very well, I'll speak to him again."

Eliza nodded. "You should, but I think the question is, what's he trying to hide? He must have a very good reason for wanting to accuse Maggie. In my experience, it means either he committed the murder, or he knows who did and wants to protect them."

The sergeant stood up. "Whatever it is, can I make myself clear? This a police matter and I don't want you meddling in it any longer."

Eliza pursed her lips. "Don't worry, Sergeant. You won't find us interfering again."

The sergeant slipped his notebook back into his breast pocket, then bid them farewell. With his back disappearing through the door, Archie stood up to follow him.

"I'll go and rescue Mrs Appleton. Wait here for me."

Moments later, Connie and Henry hurried into the dining room.

"How did it go?" Connie asked. "Did he believe you?"

"I'm not sure." Eliza's shoulders sagged. "Thankfully, Archie agreed with what I said, which certainly helped, but he clearly trusts the villagers more."

"But he can't believe Mr Stewart." Henry sat down beside her. "I don't know what's come over him. He should be defending Aunty Maggie not accusing her."

Eliza sighed. "He should, but the way he behaved in the bar suggests he knows something."

"Do you think so?" Connie's eyes were wide.

"Why else would he be so keen to lay the blame on his sister-in-law? I'm sure Jean would be furious if she found out. Anyway, Sergeant Mitchell said he'd speak to him again."

Henry let out a low whistle. "Mr Stewart didn't get any better after you left but should we really have him as a suspect?"

"I don't know. He's certainly big enough and strong

enough to have done it, but why would he want Mrs Scott dead? We need to find out more about him."

"You'll do no such thing." Archie retook his seat. "You've just told Sergeant Mitchell that you wouldn't interfere any more."

Eliza gave Archie her sweetest smile. "You weren't listening. I said he wouldn't *catch* me interfering. That's quite different."

"Eliza!"

"Eliza nothing. You saw how clueless he was. If you don't want your sister arrested, we need to find the real killer and do it quickly. Now, is there any chance of a cup of tea around here?"

Connie's face lit up. "Oh, yes, I took the liberty of ordering some while I was waiting."

"Splendid. So, Henry, do you want to tell us what you found in church this morning ... once you'd finally woken up?"

Henry rolled his eyes. "You're not going to forget that in a hurry, are you?" He pulled a piece of paper from his pocket and handed it to Eliza. "Here, I've written everything down."

"Let's see." Eliza studied the elegant cursive lettering. "So Mr Scott and Miss Davison were married in October 1852 and Robert was baptised in August 1853." She looked up at Henry. "You didn't write down how old Robert was when he was baptised."

"It wasn't recorded."

Eliza's eyes narrowed. "That's unusual."

Henry nodded. "I did wonder, but it wasn't the only entry without an age. I looked at all the entries for 1853 and there were at least half a dozen with no age."

"But Mr and Mrs Scott were listed as the parents?"

"They were."

"Eliza, surely you don't think...!" Connie stared at her friend, her mouth open.

"It was just an idea, but probably wrong." Eliza's shoulders slumped.

"You shouldn't be upset." Archie scowled. "Mr Scott's our brother-in-law. He'd be beside himself if he found out he was conceived out of wedlock."

"You're right. I shouldn't wish that on him." Eliza sat up straight as a maid brought in a tea tray and placed four cups in the centre of the table. She smiled her thanks and waited for her to leave the room. "Now, where were we?"

"We've just established there was nothing suspicious about Mr Scott's birth." Connie set each cup on its saucer.

Eliza groaned. "Oh yes."

"I do have a piece of gossip that might cheer you up, though." Henry's eyes shone.

"Go on, then, what is it?"

"Well! When I started looking at the records, I couldn't decide which year to look at and so I began in 1850."

Eliza tutted. "I'm not surprised it took you so long."

"I've already explained that. Anyway, I went through every page in the register until I found Mr Scott's baptism."

"Henry, will you stop teasing. What did you find?"

His eyes twinkled. "That in October 1851 an illegitimate baby boy was baptised, aged only three days..."

Eliza sighed. "I'm afraid it's not as uncommon as some would have us think."

"Maybe not, but the fact that the mother was none other than Miss McGovern may be of interest."

Eliza's mouth fell open, and she stared at Connie and Archie before turning back to a triumphant-looking Henry.

"Miss McGovern?" Eliza pointed towards the bar. "From down the road? Are you sure?"

"There can't be many Miss McGoverns in St Giles of the right age."

"Was there a father listed?"

"No, that's one of the reasons I noticed it. The box for his name was empty. The other thing is, I'd say that someone was trying to hide the fact. The entry for the baptism was near the top of the right-hand page of the register, but there was nothing else registered on that page. The next baptism was only a week later, but it was on the start of a new page."

Eliza chewed down on her lip. "Was the baby called Donald by any chance?"

This time it was Henry's mouth that fell open. "How on earth did you know that?"

"Oh, Eliza, surely not." Connie covered her mouth. "Do you think Mrs Scott was threatening to tell Mr Carmichael that Miss McGovern was his mother?"

"Mr Carmichael? The stranger." Henry ran a hand through his hair. "My goodness."

"It's certainly what it sounds like." Eliza glanced at the door. "We'd better keep our voices down. Something like this would ruin Miss McGovern."

"She'd be devastated if she knew we'd found out." Connie caught her breath. "You don't think she would have murdered Mrs Scott to keep her quiet?"

Eliza sat back with her hands on her face. "If I'm honest, it would surprise me. She couldn't strangle anyone..."

"It's a preposterous thought," Archie said. "I've known the woman all my life and she wouldn't hurt a fly."

"But what if she had an accomplice?" Henry's eyes glistened.

Eliza sat forward again. "That's what I'm wondering. Mrs Scott persuaded Mr Carmichael to come to the headland by promising to tell him who his parents are. What if Miss McGovern and the father found out what she was planning and got together in order to stop her?"

"But why would she do something like that now, after all this time? What did she have to gain?" Connie's eyes narrowed. "That's the bit that doesn't make sense to me."

"Nor me."

"And how did anyone know what she was up to?" Archie added. "Don't forget, as far as we can tell, she'd spoken to no one from St Giles for years."

Eliza nodded. "You're right." She picked up a teaspoon to stir the pot. "I'd suggest that if we find out who the father is, we'll go a long way to finding our killer."

"We can't just go and ask her." Connie's voice squeaked as she spoke.

"We may have no choice."

"What about asking Reverend Rennie?" Archie suggested. "People often confide in their minister when they need forgiveness."

"It was such a long time ago, though. I doubt Reverend Rennie conducted the baptism."

"No, he didn't." Henry turned over the paper Eliza still had in front of her. "The register was signed by the previous minister, Reverend Campbell."

The four of them sat in silence until Connie's eyes

brightened. "Reverend Rennie may still be able to help! He said he was on probation when he arrived. How long ago was that?"

"Goodness, Connie, you're right." Eliza flicked back through her notes. "He told us he's been reverend here for over fifty years but was on probation for two years before that. That means he'd have been at the church at the time."

Connie's cheeks glowed. "We'd better be quick with this tea, then, if we want to visit him this afternoon."

The sun was dropping behind the hill to the rear of the manse as Archie escorted the group up the front path.

"I won't come in; I promised Ma and Pa I'd call again this afternoon. I'm sure you can manage without me. I'll see you at the inn later."

Eliza waited for Archie to leave them. "Shall we try the garden first? He seems to spend most of his time out there." She strolled around the side of the house and paused when she saw the minister sitting in the shade of a large honeysuckle.

"Good afternoon. I hope you don't mind us disturbing you."

"No, of course not, my dear, come on in. All of you." He caught hold of Henry's arm as he struggled to stand up. "There are a couple of chairs by the corner of the house. Would you mind fetching them?"

"You've made a lovely job of the roses," Eliza said. "It must take a lot of time."

Reverend Rennie admired the display. "Time doesn't matter when you enjoy what you do. I've no one else to give my affection to, so the roses benefit."

"And you can tell." Eliza took the seat Henry offered while Connie sat on the bench alongside the minister.

"Now then, how may I help?"

Eliza smiled. "We're still intrigued by Mrs Scott's death and wondered if you could tell us a little more about your early years in St Giles."

"My early years? My, that will take me back. What would you like to know?"

"You told us on Sunday that you arrived here many years ago. Could you be more specific about the date?"

"Now, let me see. I took part in my very first service in April 1850, the week after Easter to be precise. I don't remember the date exactly, but Easter was early that year, at the end of March, and so it would have been the beginning of April."

"And then you were fully ordained a couple of years later?"

"Yes, in June 1852."

"Can you tell us, would you have been involved with baptisms while you were doing your probation?"

"Most certainly. It was a time of training and so I often assisted Reverend Campbell. By early 1852, I was conducting the services myself."

"What do you remember about the baptism of Miss McGovern's son in 1851?"

The colour drained from the minister's face as he glared at Henry. "You asked if you could look for information about Mrs Scott."

Henry's cheeks coloured. "And I was, but I stumbled across the baptism of a baby called Donald."

"The child you've known for years as Mr Carmichael."

Eliza didn't take her eyes from the minister, who struggled to push himself from the bench.

"I'm sorry, my dear, but I need to go."

"Please, Reverend, don't. We need the truth. We believe the death of Mrs Scott may have been related to this baptism. If we can't trust a man of God to tell us what happened, who should we ask?"

The minister had taken a few steps but stopped and turned back to face them. "That was private information then, and it is now."

"I'd agree, but as I say, it may be related to Mrs Scott's death and may help us save an innocent woman from the gallows. Please."

Reverend Rennie hesitated before nodding to himself. "It was a long time ago..."

"Perhaps you could start by telling us who was at the service."

He shook his head as he retook his seat. "Nobody. Just Reverend Campbell, Miss McGovern and the child. Even I stayed in the vestry while it took place."

"But you kept an eye on the proceedings?"

"I could hear Reverend Campbell reciting the service."

"And am I right in saying that the baby was christened Donald?"

The minister nodded.

"The same Donald who was seen loitering around the church on the day of Mrs Scott's death?"

"Yes."

Eliza's eyes flicked to Connie. "Did he tell you why he'd suddenly turned up in St Giles?"

"Yes."

Eliza chewed on her lip. "So, you knew someone had told him about his real parents. Why didn't you mention this to us?"

The minister mopped his brow with a handkerchief. "Because you'd have wanted to know more, and it wasn't my place to tell you. Miss McGovern was terribly upset by the whole affair and arranged for the baby to be adopted immediately after the baptism. I couldn't break that confidence."

"What about the father?"

"The father?" The minister shook his head. "Oh, no, she didn't tell me who he was. It wouldn't surprise me if no one knows, not even the man himself."

Eliza nodded. "I could see her doing that, but sadly we believe someone found out about the baby, and his parents, and whoever it was told Mrs Scott."

Reverend Rennie stared at her. "Well, I don't know how; it didn't come from either myself or Reverend Campbell. We even held the baptism after dark so no one would see her carrying the baby to the church."

"Could anyone have gone back through the parish records as we did?" Henry asked.

The minister put a hand to his chest. "Gracious no, not without me knowing. The book is always kept in the office with the door shut."

"But you're not always there. Have you ever suspected it had been tampered with?"

"No, never."

"All right then, can you tell us what happened after the service? You said the baby was adopted immediately. Was he taken straight from the church?"

The minister's cheeks coloured. "Reverend Campbell brought him to the manse and then the following day a man collected him to take him to the new parents."

"Do you know who this man was?"

"No. I didn't recognise him and there were no introductions. To the best of my knowledge he wasn't told who the mother was."

Eliza's eyes narrowed. "But you kept your eye on the child. How did you know where he'd been sent?"

"Reverend Campbell received a letter from the new mother thanking him. Sadly, it didn't turn out well for them, but by then we couldn't intervene. The boy was sent to Edinburgh, and I was only reintroduced to him many years later when he came back."

"And you never told Miss McGovern any of this?"

"Gracious no. Once the baby left, she drew a veil over the whole sorry episode and never spoke of it again."

Eliza nodded. "I can understand why she would want to move on. It would have been very difficult for her otherwise. While we're here, may we ask about Robert Scott? According to Henry, his age at the time of the baptism is missing from the records. It was 1853 by this stage, which means you'd have been the minister. Do you remember how old he was?"

The minister shrugged. "I can't say I do."

"Did you make a habit of omitting ages? I ask because Henry noticed they were missing on a number of other records for that year. Why would you do that?"

The reverend hesitated before waving a dismissive hand. "It was probably an oversight."

"Really?" Eliza raised an eyebrow. "Or could it have been to hide the age of the child? I'm beginning to wonder if conceiving a child out of wedlock is more common than you'd realise around here."

"What an outrageous thing to say." The colour returned to the minister's cheeks.

"And yet your protestations lack conviction." Eliza rapped her fingers on her knee. "I'm wondering if this was a lucrative sideline. Parents came to you fearing judgement from the rest of the village because the child was born less than nine months after a marriage, but in return for a generous donation to the church, you promised to leave the child's age out of the register."

The vicar's watery eyes gazed at Eliza. "Was it wrong to forgive people and let them get on with their lives without fear of recrimination? Have you any idea how quickly gossip spreads in a village like this?"

Eliza nodded. "Actually, I have, but I doubt the church would have been quite so forgiving if there hadn't been money involved."

"As I say, it was a long time ago and it stopped shortly after I was made minister. Now if that's all." Once again, he pushed himself up.

"No, not quite. Before we go, may I ask one more thing?" Eliza waited for him to sit back down. "For many of the baptisms I imagine you omitted the ages because the child had been born too early. In the case of Robert Scott, could it have been because he was older than expected?"

The minister remained silent.

"All right, let me ask it another way. Have you any reason to believe that old Mr Scott was not the father of the young baby Robert?"

"No! None at all."

"So why did they want the age omitted?"

Connie put a hand to her mouth. "Are you suggesting she was already expecting when she married Mr Scott and she wanted to hide it?"

Eliza bobbed her head from side to side. "It would make sense."

Henry nodded. "It would. Tell me, Reverend, had you heard from Mrs Scott in the last few weeks?"

"No, I'd not seen her since she left the village."

"So why would she suddenly want to embarrass Miss McGovern by revealing her secret?"

The minister shook his head. "I swear on the Bible, I don't know, but the one person who might is Miss McGovern herself."

CHAPTER TWENTY-ONE

The dining room was unusually busy for breakfast the next day, leaving little opportunity for discussion.

"What will you do this morning?" Eliza asked Archie.

"Jean's arranged a family walk on the beach for those of us who can make it. She's decided Maggie needs cheering up."

"I'd say she's right." Eliza moved in closer. "Have you heard whether she's had a visit from the police yet?"

"They hadn't been when I last saw her. That's half her trouble, not knowing when there'll be a knock on the door."

"They've no consideration. Well, send her our regards and tell her we're doing all we can."

"I'm sure she knows that already, but I will." He grinned. "I'll make sure Ma hears me, too."

Eliza rolled her eyes. "As if she's interested. Right, are we ready to go?"

With agreement all around, they made their way to the door, but Eliza shivered as it was opened. "My, it feels cool out there today."

"We are approaching the end of August. The easterly winds are starting to pick up."

Eliza pulled her shawl tight. "Well, if they wouldn't mind waiting a few more days, I'd be very grateful."

Archie put an arm around her shoulders and squeezed her. "For you, my dear, I'll see what I can do."

"Archie!" She shrugged him off. "People might see!"

"Are we walking you all the way to Miss McGovern's?" Henry tried his best to ignore his parents.

"No, you'd better not." Eliza readjusted her shawl. "If you stop before we get to the bend, we'll carry on alone. She'll be devastated when we tell her what we've found out, and if she thinks you know about it too, it will make it worse."

"Makes sense." Henry nodded.

"Oh, while I think on, ask Maggie if the solicitor told them anything else of interest after we'd left. We need to call on Mr Watson this afternoon and so if he did, it may be useful."

Miss McGovern gave Eliza and Connie a wave as they approached the house and stood up as they walked through the garden gate.

"What a nice surprise." She smiled as she opened the front door.

Eliza returned her smile. "May we come in?"

"Most certainly. I'm always glad of the company."

Eliza fidgeted with her fingers as Miss McGovern fussed about the chairs and poured them each a cup of tea.

"Now then, my dears, is this a social call?"

"Actually, we've come on a rather delicate matter." Eliza held the old woman's gaze. "Something you'll find upsetting."

"Is it to do with Mrs Scott's death?"

"It is. But it also concerns you."

Miss McGovern studied the table and reached down to wipe away an invisible mark.

"The thing is–" Eliza took a deep breath "–we had reason to look through the parish register yesterday and came across an entry that surprised us."

"Oh yes?" Miss McGovern's voice faltered.

"In 1851 there was a baptism for a baby boy called Donald. You were recorded as his mother."

Miss McGovern's face turned white as she put a hand to her chest.

"We understand it must be a shock to have this brought up after so long, and we wouldn't mention it if it wasn't important, but we believe Donald may be the reason Mrs Scott was murdered."

"Donald was?" Her voice cracked. "Why?"

Eliza shook her head. "We've no evidence yet, but we suspect Mrs Scott found out he was your son and was threatening to give him your details."

Miss McGovern gasped. "No! How could she?"

"We were hoping you might be able to tell us."

Miss McGovern leaned back in her chair, her mind clearly not in the room. "Why would she do such a thing? I hardly knew the woman."

"What about when you were young? Did you socialise together then?" Eliza waited for a response that didn't come. "Miss McGovern?"

Miss McGovern blinked and glanced at Eliza before turning her attention back to the window. "We went to the same social events when we were girls, but she was always one for the boys. I didn't spend a lot of time with her."

"Could you tell us who did?"

"As I said, it was the boys from the village. Most of them, in fact. She always liked to be the centre of attention. She was very pretty back then."

"Have you any idea how she might have found out about the baby?"

"No, none." Pain was etched across her face. "I didn't realise myself for months after ... you know, and as soon as it became obvious, Ma spotted it and confined me to the house. She was so disgusted she couldn't even look at me, and nobody else saw me after that."

"Did you consider marrying the baby's father?"

Miss McGovern let out a hysterical laugh. "There wasn't a chance. We hadn't even been walking out with each other; it was just a brief liaison when I'd been given too much gin. He'd been chasing me for months, but once he got his way, that was it." Her voice dropped. "I must have been a real disappointment. I didn't bother with men after that."

Eliza glanced at Connie before taking a sip of tea. *How do you follow that?* She placed her cup back on its saucer. "Can we go back to who else may have known? Obviously Reverend Campbell, the old minister, and Reverend Rennie, who was doing his probation at the time. Perhaps they told someone."

"Oh no, they were the height of discretion. Reverend Campbell even took Donald from me after the baptism and said he'd found a home for him with a childless family."

"*He* found a family for him?" Eliza's eyebrows rose. "Reverend Rennie told us you'd arranged the adoption."

Miss McGovern shook her head. "He must be mistaken. Reverend Campbell told me it was for the best if I gave him up quickly, and so he took him from me there and then. I can't deny I was sorry to see him go, but with things as they were, it was the answer to a prayer. After that, Reverend Campbell offered me a job as live-in housekeeper at the manse. I think it was to keep an eye on me so I wouldn't go off the rails again, but I didn't mind. It got me away from Ma, who never forgave me. I stayed when Reverend Rennie moved in and only came home once Ma died."

"Did Reverend Campbell tell you what happened to Donald?"

"Not a word. He said I needed to make a clean break. Not that I didn't wonder; I hope he's had a happy life."

Connie leaned forward and put her cup and saucer onto the table. "If Reverend Campbell organised the adoption himself, might he have passed your details to anyone? The new parents perhaps."

"Not at all. They had no business knowing."

"Maybe not, but could he have told them, anyway?"

"No, he wouldn't." Miss McGovern continued to stare out of the window.

"May I ask who delivered the baby then?" Eliza kept her eyes on Miss McGovern. "Could a doctor or midwife have told anyone about it?"

Miss McGovern sighed. "No, as I said, Ma was so ashamed of me she delivered him herself ... and I'm certain she didn't breathe a word of it. She wouldn't even arrange the baptism because she was too embarrassed. If she'd had her way, the poor mite wouldn't have been baptised at all."

"So you arranged it with Reverend Campbell yourself?"

"I did. Two days after the birth. I can still remember it. I was only seventeen and so shy."

Eliza tapped her pencil on her chin. "This is just a

thought, but did you visit the manse or the church when you spoke to the minister?"

Miss McGovern turned her head towards Eliza. "The church. Why?"

"I'm wondering if you were seen going in ... or overheard while you were there. You'd have attracted some interest if you hadn't been around for four or five months."

Miss McGovern stared at Eliza, her mouth open.

"Did you see someone?" Eliza said.

"I didn't, but I do remember feeling very conspicuous when I was in the church ... as if someone was watching from the shadows. I put it down to feeling guilty."

"Did you have the same feeling at the baptism itself?"

Confusion crossed Miss McGovern's face. "No, actually, I didn't. Do you think someone was watching that first meeting?"

"Someone who overheard and told Mrs Scott?" Connie asked.

"What if it was Mrs Scott herself?" Eliza's eyes sparkled.

Miss McGovern gasped. "If it was her, why wait so long to tell anyone? In fact, why say anything at all? She'd no reason to dislike me."

"You're sure?"

"Well ... yes."

Eliza made a note on the paper in front of her. "We need to be certain about this because if you knew Mrs Scott was about to reveal your secret, it's quite a motive for murder."

"What do you mean?" Miss McGovern put her hands on the arm of her chair as if to stand up but collapsed back into the cushions. "I wouldn't kill anyone."

"No, but if she was about to tell Donald about you and his

father, it could be considered a reason for either of you to silence her. My fear is that as a woman, you'd have the most to lose by this information being made public."

"But that's nonsense. I'd no idea she knew. I didn't think anyone did. How could I possibly suspect she was about to tell anyone?"

"Had she visited or written to you lately?

"No. As I've said, we weren't close."

Eliza pursed her lips. "In that case, could it have been the father she wanted to cause trouble for, rather than you?"

"No." Miss McGovern was adamant. "I've never told anyone who it was. Not a soul. She couldn't possibly have known."

"Did the father know about the baby?" Connie suggested.

"No. And it's going to stay that way."

Eliza nodded. "Very well. We'll leave it like that for now, but if we think the father was somehow involved in the murder, you'll have to tell someone."

"Why would he be?" Miss McGovern asked. "She couldn't be blackmailing him over fathering a child out of wedlock. Firstly, he wouldn't believe her, because he didn't know, and secondly, men have been getting away with that sort of behaviour for years. Nobody bats an eyelid."

Connie sighed. "She's right."

"Well, there's got to be something." Eliza scratched her head. "Perhaps there was more to it than that. What about Mrs Scott's confinement when she was having her son?" She flicked back through her notes. "We've been told she was betrothed to Mr Watson but without warning left him and married Mr Scott within two months. The date of birth for the baby wasn't recorded in the parish records. Miss McGovern, do you remember anything about that?"

A look of recognition crossed Miss McGovern's face. "Now you mention it, there were rumours at the time."

A smile flicked across Eliza's lips. *Is this why Ma and Pa Thomson refused to talk to me?* "Could you give us any more details?"

Miss McGovern shifted in her seat. "Very well. If I remember rightly, the boy was born about six or seven months after she married Mr Scott, but one morning I heard her discussing the baptism with Reverend Rennie. I worked at the manse by then, if you remember. She said Robert was a small baby and had been born early. I presume that was what she told everyone because before long that was the story the whole village believed."

"Did he look small to you?"

Miss McGovern's brow creased. "Do you know, I don't actually remember seeing him. Not properly, at any rate. He was always under layers of blankets in his pram. I never once saw her hold him."

I wonder. Eliza's brow furrowed. "Did you or anyone else suspect it was Mr Watson's child?"

"Mr Watson's?" Miss McGovern spluttered. "Good grief, of course not. The early rumours suggested that Miss Davison had secretly been having a liaison with Mr Scott while she'd been engaged to Mr Watson. Once she found out she was in the family way, she rushed off to marry the father."

"That makes sense." Connie nodded.

"It does, but was there any suspicion she was seeing Mr Scott while she was with Mr Watson?"

"Oh no." Miss McGovern folded her hands on her lap. "She kept that very quiet."

"And she always insisted that Mr Scott was the father?"

Miss McGovern shrugged. "As I say, I didn't really speak to her, but as far as I'm aware, there was nothing to suggest he wasn't."

CHAPTER TWENTY-TWO

Archie and Henry were waiting outside the church by the time Eliza and Connie left Miss McGovern's.

Eliza waved when she saw them. "How did you know to wait here for us? I thought you'd be at the inn."

Henry laughed. "We called in but when you weren't there, we decided to walk up for you, but you were deep in conversation with Miss McGovern."

"Good grief." Eliza gasped. "You mean we were so engrossed we didn't notice you?"

Connie's cheeks coloured. "I hope we didn't miss anything going on outside."

"I presume you've had a productive morning." Archie offered Eliza his arm before they started walking. "You were there long enough."

Eliza sighed. "Not as much as I'd have liked, to be honest. She refuses to tell anyone who the father is and said that she's never told a soul. There's no way Mrs Scott could have known."

"But did she have any idea how Mrs Scott found out that she was the mother?"

"No. She's under the impression the whole affair was a secret between herself, her ma and the Reverends Campbell and Rennie."

"How can she be so sure the clergy didn't tell anyone?"

Eliza shrugged. "She trusts them implicitly. We did make her wonder if someone had overheard her arranging the baptism with Reverend Campbell, though. She said the church felt strange at the time but put it down to her guilty conscience. Now she's not so sure."

Archie grimaced. "But that's not likely to stand up in court."

"You're right." Eliza paused while Archie opened the door to the inn. "Did you find out anything else from Maggie?"

"No. Her and Ma are becoming increasingly worried that the police still think she did it. But the solicitor refused to give any more details."

Eliza groaned. "So, it will all come down to what Mr Watson tells us about the solicitor's letters this afternoon. We need something to eat first, and then we can walk over once he leaves the inn."

It was almost three o'clock when they left The Coach House, and the gulls were circling overhead as they walked once more up to Clifftop House.

"I won't miss this climb when we get back to Moreton." Eliza hung onto Archie's arm for assistance. "It's the worst thing about St Giles."

"I'm sure you said that last time we came." Connie smirked at her friend.

Eliza groaned as they approached the top. "Well, I obviously meant it."

Henry laughed. "It's good for you, Mother. Stop your moaning."

They paused at the top before heading towards the house where Archie knocked on the front door. Eliza had counted to ten by the time it was opened.

"Oh, it's you." Mr Watson stood with an arm across the door barring their entry.

"Might we have a word?" Archie asked.

"Haven't we had enough words? Every time I see you, it's something else."

"We've learned some new information that only you can help with." Eliza returned his stare. "May we come in?"

With a second's pause, Mr Watson stepped back. "If you must, but you've got five minutes. I'm going out shortly."

Mr Watson remained standing as the ladies took a seat around the now familiar kitchen table. "What is it this time?"

"We've been told that Mrs Scott wanted to buy Clifftop House." Archie's voice was authoritative, but Mr Watson only shrugged.

"She may have wanted to buy it, but it's not for sale."

"So, is that what she came to see you about?" Eliza asked.

Mr Watson closed his eyes and took a deep breath. "How many times must I tell you, I haven't seen her for over twenty years?"

"All right, can you explain why her solicitor told us he's written to you on several occasions, but he's had no response from you? Did you receive the letters?"

"Oh yes, I received them, and I wrote back twice to tell her I wasn't interested."

Eliza stared at him. "Your replies seem to have bypassed the solicitor."

Mr Watson's jaw clenched. "I didn't send them to him, I wrote directly to her. She mustn't have passed them on."

Henry walked towards him. "If the solicitor wrote to you, why not reply to him?"

"Because I wanted to make sure the stupid woman got the message first-hand without any solicitor changing my words."

"When did you send these letters?" Eliza asked.

Mr Watson shrugged. "Over the last couple of weeks; I don't remember exactly."

"And it didn't occur to you to tell us about them?"

"You didn't ask. You asked if I'd seen her, and I hadn't."

"I also asked if she'd written to you, which you denied."

"She hadn't written to me; it was her solicitor."

Eliza's face was scarlet. "You've managed to twist every question we've asked to the point I don't think we can believe a word you say." She stood up and paced to the far side of the room before turning back, her face fierce. "You know what I think happened? That she came to see you last Thursday and you argued. That's why you didn't mention it, because it would have provided a perfect motive for murdering her."

Mr Watson raised his face to the ceiling and muttered something under his breath. "Watch my lips. I did not see her on Thursday ... I've not seen her for over twenty years. I'd written to tell her the house wasn't for sale and told her not to bother calling because she wasn't welcome. Now, if you wouldn't mind leaving, I've things to do."

Mr Watson marched to the door, but Eliza stayed where she was.

"One more thing before we go. How well do you know Miss McGovern?"

Mr Watson turned and stared at her. "Miss McGovern? I know she's the old dear from down the road, but she keeps to herself. I've not spoken to her in years."

Eliza stared at him. "How many years?"

"I don't know." He flapped his arms while he struggled for the right words. "Fifty probably. Yes, at least that. Since before I was married. Now if you wouldn't mind, I'm going out."

Archie's back foot had barely crossed the threshold when Mr Watson slammed the door behind them. With a start, Connie blew out her cheeks. "Well, that didn't go according to plan."

"No, it didn't." Eliza stopped and stared back at the house. "Would you say the fact he was rather cross means he's hiding something? Perhaps we're getting close to the truth."

"For goodness' sake, Eliza." Archie stepped past her to open the gate. "Don't you ever know when to stop?"

"I do, as it happens, but now is not the time." Eliza paused again once she'd passed through the gate. "If he's going out shortly, I suggest we come back for a look around."

"What on earth are you hoping to find?"

"I don't know. We could start by seeing if he can get to the path along the cliff without having to come out this way. There's got to be some clues to tell us what happened between her leaving the bench and ending up on the beach."

"We could sit on the bench and take in the view," Connie suggested.

"That's a splendid idea. We might get a better sense of what Mrs Scott saw while she was there."

210

The breeze was cool as they sat down, and Eliza and Connie pulled their shawls more tightly around their shoulders.

"It's not that bad." Archie pointed up to the clouds. "They're moving quickly enough, and the sun should be out again shortly. Besides, you should be thankful it's dry. It wouldn't have been as pleasant traipsing around the village in the rain."

"No, that's true. And the views are spectacular." Eliza gazed over to her right-hand side and studied Clifftop House. "The house does have the best position in the village and the path down the cliff runs directly behind it. I wonder if there's a gate that Mr Watson can use without the need to leave by the front door."

"If there isn't, I'm sure I'd put one in." Henry stood up. "Shall I go and look?"

"Not yet. Sit down and wait until he's gone." Eliza glanced over her shoulder. "He seems to be taking his time given he was in a hurry."

Archie tutted. "He can't just leave when he wants to. If he has to sort the horses out, it will take him a while."

Henry pointed to a gap in the bushes. "There he is. That must be the stables at the back."

Eliza followed Henry's gaze. "I wonder where he's going. It's quite late in the day to be attaching the carriage."

"Into St Andrews I would imagine," Archie said. "He wouldn't take his own carriage if he was planning to take a train."

"Ah, there he goes." Henry stood up as the carriage travelled along the side of the house to the road. "It must have been ready."

"Will you sit down and wait until he's gone." Eliza pulled on his jacket. "We don't want to attract attention."

A minute later, once Mr Watson had driven off towards St Andrews, Henry scurried towards the back of the house and disappeared down the path to the cliff. When he didn't come back, Archie stood up. "I'd better go after him."

"Wait for us." Eliza extended her hand for him to pull her up. "We might as well walk with you to save you coming back."

They followed Henry's footsteps, and before long saw him on the other side of the hedge.

"How did you get over there?" Eliza asked.

"You were right. There's an entrance at the far end."

They followed the path and came to an old iron gate, which Eliza pushed, causing it to glide open.

"I'd say this is used regularly. It wouldn't open like that if it wasn't, it'd be seized up with rust."

"He told us he didn't use the path though," Connie said.

"He did, but can we believe anything he says?" Eliza let herself into the back garden and wandered over to Henry. "Have you found anything?"

Henry shook his head. "Nothing."

"Can we get into the stables?"

Archie walked to the wooden structure and opened the door. "It all looks perfectly normal, although even if Mrs Scott was here, it's almost certainly been cleaned out since."

Eliza followed him inside and turned through a full circle. "Yes, you're right, there's nothing here."

Archie closed the stable door as Henry led them back to the gate. "He can get into Mr Burns' garden here." He pointed to another gate in the corner where the two properties joined.

"Ah, look at those plants." Connie pointed to a patch of wilted evergreens just beyond the gate. "I don't suppose they're used to it being so dry up here."

"Less of your cheek." Archie gave her a mock scowl. "We don't get nearly as much rain on this side of the country as they do in Glasgow. It's quite dry here, even in the winter."

Connie's cheeks flushed. "I'm sorry ... but surely that means Mr Burns should have known to water them?"

Archie laughed. "No apology needed; most people have the impression it does nothing but rain in Scotland, but they're wrong. And yes, Mr Burns should know better."

"Well, I hope Sergeant Cooper's watering the plants for us." Connie smiled as she mentioned their local police officer. "I don't suppose Moreton's had much rain while we've been here."

"Or any murders to keep Sergeant Cooper busy. Now, I'm sure the plants will be thriving when we get home. Come along." An air of impatience crept into Eliza's voice. "We've only got two days to solve this murder before we leave."

The bar was empty when they arrived at The Coach House, and Eliza and Connie wandered over to the table in the back corner adjacent to the fireplace.

"It mustn't be as late as I thought." She glanced at the grandfather clock near the door. "Still not four o'clock. At least we can sit and have a cup of tea without being disturbed. I'm tired of being in the dining room." Eliza took a seat where she could see the whole room and lifted her bag onto her knee to retrieve her notes. She was about to put it back on the floor when she noticed a man sitting in the dimly lit corner opposite. "Mr Stewart, is that you? What are you doing here?"

"I was enjoying a bit of peace and quiet." Mr Stewart

picked up his tankard and sauntered over to them. "You're here for afternoon tea, are you?"

"We are. We're not having much success finding Mrs Scott's killer and so sometimes it helps to take a break."

"Isn't Dr Thomson with you?"

Eliza glanced over to the door. "He's just ordering some tea. He won't be long."

Mr Stewart pulled up a stool. "Who've you been talking to today then?"

"Mrs Appleton and I called on Miss McGovern this morning and we're all just back from Mr Watson's."

"Mr Watson? Why did you need to talk to him again?"

Eliza shuddered as Mr Stewart glared at her. "We found out some new information we hoped he could help with."

"And could he?" Mr Stewart leaned forward.

"No." Eliza shook her head. "I'm afraid we're at a dead end."

"So, will you leave it to the police now? Or do I have to tell them you're still interfering?"

"Why would you do that?" Eliza's eyes narrowed as she studied him. "Do you have something to hide?"

"Don't be ridiculous; I just want a proper job done. Women can't do police work."

"This one can." Archie walked up behind Mr Stewart and took the seat beside him. "In fact, I'd say she and Mrs Appleton are doing a far better job than the police. If I'm not mistaken, they still think Maggie's responsible. Surely you want us to prove them wrong?"

"Oh ... yes, of course. T-that's a terrible business."

"Can I ask how well *you* knew old Mrs Scott?" Eliza asked him.

Mr Stewart's moustache twitched. "Not at all, really. I was introduced to her when I first met Jean, but shortly afterwards she moved away, and I didn't see her again."

"Did Maggie or Mr Scott ever talk about her?"

Mr Stewart laughed. "They never stopped talking about her. Not recently, anyway, and if I'm being honest, Maggie didn't have a good word to say about her. You can't blame the police for assuming she had it in for her."

"Not when half the village keeps reminding them. Why doesn't anyone suspect Mr Scott?"

"Robert? He wouldn't have done it. He just got on with the job of looking after his ma. You didn't hear him criticising her like Maggie did."

"And yet Mr Scott didn't like his father."

Mr Stewart sucked air through his teeth. "He hated him, but even then, he didn't murder him. I've never seen anyone look so relieved to be told their pa was dead."

Eliza cocked her head to one side. "Do you know why?"

"Nope, he never told me."

Archie held the gaze of his brother-in-law. "I don't remember there being a problem when he married Maggie. Did you know about it then?"

"Nobody did. It only came out when the old man died." Mr Stewart put his empty tankard on the table. "Anyway, nice to talk but I need to go. The boys'll be moaning that I've not done my share of the nets."

Archie stood up to see him out. "I must admit, I'm surprised you're still here with all the work you need to do. I thought you usually left with the others."

"It depends on the day and the weather. If I need to get back and help the boys, I will, but if it's like today, they can manage without me. I'm usually last to leave because I don't always get here of an evening."

"Do the rest of the men leave together?" Eliza asked.

"Those that go down the hill usually walk together."

"And you walked with them last Thursday?"

Mr Stewart studied her. "I seem to remember, I told you I'd walked with Mr Cargill. Don't you have it in your notes?"

"So I do." Eliza raised her eyes to meet his. "But I don't recall making a note of whether Mr Watson and Mr Burns left with you."

Mr Stewart shrugged. "I don't remember. You'll have to ask them. Now if you'll excuse me, I've things to do."

Eliza sat back as Mr Stewart disappeared through the door.

"He knows something." She gazed at Archie as he left the building. "You were right when you said he was here later than usual. Do you think he could have been waiting for us to find out what we've been up to?"

"Why would he do that?"

"Because he knows who the killer is, and he wants to warn them if he thinks we're getting too close for his liking."

Archie shook his head. "He's part of the family, why would he help someone who's caused us so much distress?"

"Because he has other loyalties." Eliza let her thoughts wander before she sat up straight. "Henry, are you likely to see Niall and Ross this evening?"

"We've arranged to meet here for a drink later."

"All right." She paused. "Can you go and tell them that you can't make it? Say ... say we have things to do, because I think I've worked out who the murderer is."

Henry's brows drew together. "Have you?"

Eliza reached for her notes. "I need to read through these again, but I've suddenly had an idea who did it. We just need to check a few details at the church and then drive over to St Andrews."

"Who is it?" Henry's eyes were wide as Archie and Connie stared at her.

"I'll tell you later. Go and see Niall and Ross first."

Henry jumped from his seat.

"Oh, and Henry, when you speak to them, make sure Mr Stewart hears you."

CHAPTER TWENTY-THREE

I t was almost eight o'clock by the time Sergeant Mitchell stood opposite the bar in The Coach House, waiting for the villagers to arrive. Eliza and Connie sat at a table to his right.

"That's it, come on in." He waved people in. "Leave the seats for the ladies."

Archie walked into the room with his mother on his arm and his pa following them.

"Ladies shouldn't even be in a place like this." Mrs Thomson glared at Eliza as Archie steered her past their table.

"It's perfectly acceptable under the circumstances, Ma. Why don't you sit by the window, away from the bar?"

"It might be in London..."

"All right, enough now. This is the biggest room in the village, so we have no choice. I'll order some tea to make you feel more at home. Jean, Maggie, will you sit with her?"

Eliza watched Mr Scott pat Maggie's hand before she crossed the room but became distracted when Mr Carmichael arrived with Constable McIntyre. Instinctively, her eyes flicked around the assembled crowd and she nodded to herself. *Yes, I think so.*

With the ladies at the tables and most of the men by the bar, Sergeant Mitchell turned to Eliza. "Are they all here?"

Eliza had been counting the people in. "I would say so."

"Excellent." He stepped into the middle of the room. "Now ladies and gentlemen, I imagine you're wondering why we're here at this hour on a Wednesday evening. Well, to save you all from guessing, I can tell you we have an announcement to make regarding the death of Mrs Scott. Much against my better judgement, Mrs Thomson here–" he turned and gestured towards Eliza "–has been making her own enquiries into the murder..."

"Disgraceful." A shiver ran down Eliza's back as the whole room muttered in agreement with her mother-in-law.

"Well, yes." Sergeant Mitchell nodded. "But disgraceful or not, I'm delighted to say she's now convinced us she knows the identity of our murderer." There was a gasp in the room followed by a movement of heads as everyone studied their neighbour. "If you'll give her your attention, she promises to tell you what happened."

"Thank you, Sergeant." Eliza stood up and beckoned Mr Carmichael forward. "Before we go any further, I'd like to introduce Mr Carmichael, the man some of you saw on the day of Mrs Scott's death. When we were first alerted to him, everyone thought he was a stranger, but that turned out not to be the case. In fact, Mrs Scott had recently met him, and Reverend Rennie has known him for many years."

Reverend Rennie smiled as all eyes turned to him.

"Mr Watson, you said you'd seen someone outside the

church on the afternoon Mrs Scott disappeared. Would you agree it was Mr Carmichael?"

Mr Watson looked the man up and down. "I would say so."

"And Mrs Baker, may I ask you the same question?"

Mrs Baker turned to her husband before nodding. "I'd recognise that oversized jacket anywhere."

"Excellent." Eliza gave her a warm smile.

"This is the man I saw, too." Miss McGovern's cheeks flushed as she spoke, and Eliza placed a reassuring hand on her shoulder.

"May I also ask, did any of you see Mr Carmichael with Mrs Scott?" When each of them shook their heads, Eliza nodded. "Good, so with that confirmed, where do we begin?

"If we go back to the events of last Thursday, you'll remember Mr Scott went to Cupar to collect his mother and bring her here. At the time, it was believed that nobody outside the family knew she was in St Giles. She hadn't been in the village long before she asked her daughter-in-law, Mrs Maggie Scott, if she'd take a walk with her. When they left home, Maggie thought Mrs Scott wanted to visit the shop, but it turned out that she'd made arrangements to meet Mr Carmichael on the headland."

Everyone studied Mr Carmichael with renewed interest.

"Unfortunately, shortly before quarter past two, when Mr Carmichael arrived, Mrs Scott was nowhere to be seen. This puzzled me. Only that morning, Mrs Scott had visited Mr Carmichael in St Andrews specifically to ask him to meet her there at that time. Why would she do that if she had no intention of being there? Part of the answer, I believe, is that she hadn't planned on leaving the bench."

Eliza paused as a murmur rippled through the room. "Precisely. So, who knew that Mrs Scott was in the village? The fact we're in holiday season and the roads were quiet actually makes this question easier to answer than it might have been. Firstly, there was Mr Scott. He'd brought his ma home at around half past one that afternoon and had stayed in the house until about three o'clock. I can confirm he did get home at that time as I was at the house with my family when they arrived." She indicated to Archie and Henry, who stood by the bar. "We left the house at approximately quarter to two and called on Mr and Mrs Stewart. We then returned to The Coach House at about half past three, where we met Mr and Mrs Scott who, by then, had realised old Mrs Scott was missing."

Eliza waited as Archie nodded his confirmation to the men around him. "So, what about Maggie Scott? She clearly knew her mother-in-law was here and had walked her up to the bench on the headland. As a result, she is the last person known to have seen her alive."

The murmurs started again, but Eliza held up a hand. "Please, if I may continue. I know there have been those who have speculated that Maggie had the motive and an opportunity to murder Mrs Scott, but Mrs Baker can confirm she was in the shop until around twenty-five past two and Mr Carmichael saw her leave the shop and return to the headland. When she realised Mrs Scott was no longer there, she became rather distressed and headed off towards St Andrews to look for her before returning to the headland. That was when she met Mr Scott."

Eliza noticed Mr Stewart make eye contact with the men

around him. "All right, so we can eliminate Maggie from our list of suspects, but who else saw Mrs Scott?"

"What about him?" Mr Stewart pointed to Mr Carmichael. "He was clearly on the headland at the right time."

"He was, but as I said he had gone to meet Mrs Scott. She had something she wanted to tell him, something he was desperate to hear, but unfortunately, she'd disappeared by the time he arrived. As our previous witnesses have already confirmed, nobody saw the two of them together."

"How can we be sure he's telling the truth about when he arrived?"

Eliza held up a hand to silence Mr Stewart. "That's where Miss McGovern comes in."

The elderly woman shrank into her chair as all eyes studied her.

"For those of you who don't know, from her front room Miss McGovern has a splendid view over the headland. On the day in question, she watched Maggie bring Mrs Scott to the bench before she disappeared back towards the shop. Maggie hadn't been gone more than a couple of minutes when Mrs Scott got up and apparently followed her."

"Ah, so it could have been her!" Constable McIntyre pointed at Maggie.

Eliza took a deep breath. "No, because as I've said, Mrs Baker confirmed she was in the shop by that time and Mr Carmichael saw her leave twenty or so minutes later. Now, where was I? Oh yes, by the time Mr Carmichael arrived, around quarter past two, Mrs Scott had left the bench. He was clearly looking for someone when he arrived."

Miss McGovern nodded her approval at the details.

"So that leaves us with one other person who definitely saw Mrs Scott. Mr Burns. He admitted to leaving the inn with Mr Watson sometime between two o'clock and half past. Given we know that Mrs Scott left her seat on the headland between five past and ten past two, that gives us a more precise time for when that would have been."

"If they left the inn together, why did only Mr Burns see her and not Mr Watson as well?" Mr Baker asked.

Eliza smiled. "An excellent question and one I asked myself when I learned that Mr Burns and Mr Watson spent the afternoon working together. One option is that Mr Watson lied about not seeing her. It's still a possibility, but having spoken to him on several occasions, I actually believe he didn't."

"Alleluia!" Mr Watson couldn't hide his sarcasm.

"The other option..." Eliza glared at Mr Watson as his friend patted him on the back. "...is that Mr Burns was alone when Maggie and Mrs Scott walked past him. By his own admission, he confirmed he left Mr Watson on the way home to collect some paperwork, and by the time he continued on to Clifftop House, Mr Watson had gone indoors."

"So..." Eliza paused for effect "...Mr Burns had the opportunity to murder Mrs Scott, but why would he?"

"Why would I indeed?" Mr Burns was on his feet. "This was nothing to do with me!"

"Please, Mr Burns, take your seat. That was my first thought, too. Why would Mr Burns, or for that matter any of the men in the village, want to murder a woman they hadn't seen in over twenty years?"

Eliza let the question hang as she took a sip of water. "There was no logical explanation for it. At least not based on anything that's happened recently, which made me wonder if this murder was because of some past grievance. Possibly as long as fifty years ago, when Mr Burns, Mr Watson and the fishermen of the village were all young men. What happened all those years ago that still had ramifications today?"

CHAPTER TWENTY-FOUR

E liza didn't miss the glances across the bar as she waited once more for the noise to subside. Many of those present were old enough to recall the early 1850s and mention of it had clearly revived memories.

Eliza coughed to clear her throat. "If I may continue. Many of you will remember that Mr Watson and Miss Davison, as Mrs Scott was then, were once betrothed."

There were nods around the room, but Mr Watson rubbed a hand over his eyes. "Do we have to go over this again?"

"I'm afraid so, because the fact that Miss Davison left you in the way she did has a bearing on what happened here last week."

"I hope you're not accusing me of murdering her. I've told you, I don't know why she left."

"And that's the thing." Eliza scanned the room. "Why would she walk out on a man she clearly loved, months before her marriage, when he was in the process of buying her the house she dreamed of?"

Mr Watson waved a hand dismissively. "You tell me."

Eliza smiled. "Thank you, I will. I have a theory about why she did what she did, but if anyone knows the actual turn of events, please feel free to speak up." When no one interrupted, Eliza looked over to Mr Watson. "In your younger days, I believe you played the church organ."

"What on earth's that got to do with Mrs Scott's death?" Mr Watson's face creased as he looked at his friends.

"Quite a lot, I fear. When Mrs Appleton and I first visited the church, one of the things we commented on were the recesses in the walls. They're so deep it's difficult to see the artefacts displayed within them. As this investigation proceeded, I began to wonder if they were big enough for a person to hide in."

Mr Watson shook his head. "Does it matter?"

"Oh, most definitely. So much so that before we came here tonight, I took Mrs Appleton and my son Henry into church to test the theory. With the candles giving out virtually no light, we confirmed it would be very easy for someone to hide." Eliza strolled across the front of the fireplace. "Now, that's important because Miss Davison was very much in love with Mr Watson, and speaking to the people who knew her, I got the impression she was a rather vivacious young woman..."

"Ma was?" Mr Scott's mouth dropped open.

"Indeed." Eliza looked to the bar. "I'd even go so far as to say that most of the gentlemen here would confirm that." There were several nods before she continued. "So, given the way she felt about you, Mr Watson, I believe I'm right in saying she would often pop into church to watch you practising the organ without any regard for who saw her."

Mr Watson gave a subtle nod of the head.

"I suspect that one particular afternoon, she came to see you, but you weren't there. She probably didn't think too much of it, but as she headed back to the door, she heard someone go into the office with the minister. Reverend Campbell it was then. Always one for a bit of gossip, Miss Davison hid in the nearest recess and overheard a very private conversation."

Miss McGovern squirmed in her seat, but all eyes were on Mr Watson.

"You don't know that."

"Not for certain, no, which is why I'm happy for anyone to correct me, but having spoken to a number of people this week, I believe Mrs Scott heard a very distressed young woman arranging a baptism for a baby she'd had out of wedlock."

Eliza paused as murmurs once again filled the room, and Sergeant Mitchell stepped forward.

"Can we have quiet, please?"

Eliza nodded as the noise abated. "The thing is, Miss Davison undoubtedly recognised the voice of the woman concerned. She also heard that the child would be adopted."

Mr Watson shrugged to the men at the bar. "I'm sorry, you've lost me now. What has this got to do with her death?"

Eliza clasped her hands to her chest. "We're coming to that. You see, I've heard that around that time, you ran a lot of errands for Reverend Campbell. Being in the church as often as you were meant the two of you were on good terms, and one of the things you took charge of was finding homes for unwanted babies. It was straightforward really. You'd come across several unmarried mothers who couldn't keep their children and had made it your business to find couples desperate to adopt. All you had to do was match them up, set your price and take their money. After all, what harm were you doing? You were giving the unmarried mother another chance in life, while at the same time easing a couple's pain at being childless. On top of all that, you split the money between yourself and Reverend Campbell. It seemed that everyone benefitted and what a splendid way to earn the extra money you needed to buy the house on the clifftop for your betrothed."

"You're talking nonsense. Selling a baby wouldn't have bought Clifftop House ... I worked hard."

"Oh, you certainly did that." Eliza's eyes were steely as she swung back to face him. "Once you realised how lucrative the business could be, you wanted more babies, but where would you find them? A village this size wasn't big enough, particularly when Reverend Rennie took over and wasn't quite so keen on your little scheme. That was when you decided to extend your business to St Andrews. There were many more unmarried mothers for you to take advantage of down there. And yes, we've checked with the old churchwarden in St Andrews. You were a regular visitor there for many years. I imagine that being so well known in church circles; it was easy enough to persuade the minister to tell you about enough children to give you a steady income."

Mr Watson banged a hand on the bar. "So, what if I did house these children? They were unwanted; I was doing everyone a favour. There was no crime to it."

Eliza softened her voice as Mr Carmichael's stature shrank. "No, maybe not an unlawful crime, but quite possibly a moral one. You didn't ask any questions of the couples you sold the babies to, did you? All you were interested in was how much money they had. If the child ultimately suffered, it was of no consequence to you because you already had the money and the house on the cliff."

Mr Watson's head sank. "It wasn't like that, we wanted what was best for them."

Mr Burns put a hand on his friend's shoulder as he glared at Eliza. "Was this really necessary? The man's done nothing wrong and I fail to see what this has to do with Mrs Scott's death."

"Ah, yes, Mrs Scott." Eliza continued to pace the floor in front of the fire. "As I said, there was one particular day that she overheard the discussion about the adoption and realised she knew the mother. It was probably of little consequence to her at the time, just a piece of gossip she could keep until later, but then two things happened that changed everything. Firstly, she learned that the man she was about to marry had once spent an illicit evening with the woman in question; secondly, she jumped to the conclusion that the child was his. In her mind, this would have raised a bigger question: did he know about it?" She stopped to stare at Mr Watson.

"Me?" The confusion on Mr Watson's face appeared genuine. "I haven't fathered any children."

Eliza studied him. "Given that Miss Davison gave you no explanation as to why she left, I believe she decided that not only were you the father, but that you knew about it. This then started a series of events that led us to where we are today. If you knew you'd fathered a child and yet were prepared to sell it, what would happen if she found out she was with child? The thought of having it taken from her must have terrified her to the point that she began to question how well she knew you."

"This is all guesswork..."

"Perhaps it is, but it isn't without foundation. I believe that once she came to this realisation, she panicked, not least because at about the same time she suspected that she too could be in the family way. Fearing the same predicament as the woman she'd overheard, she couldn't risk staying with you if it meant you'd sell her baby."

"I would never have done that. We were due to be married two months after she left."

"By which time her condition would have been obvious. No, I'm afraid that despite what you say, she felt she could no longer trust you and rushed into the arms of a man who'd adored her from afar. The unsuspecting Mr Scott. They were married before anyone realised what was happening and, most importantly, before *he* knew she was indeed expecting another man's child."

"Is this me you're talking about?" Robert Scott's eyes were wide. "You mean that man wasn't my father?"

"That's my belief." Eliza paused to let Mr Scott take in the news.

He shook his head, disbelief etched across his face before he stared at Eliza. "That makes so much sense."

"Doesn't it?" Eliza flicked her eyes from Mr Watson to Mr Scott. "The man you thought of as your father had mistreated you since the day you were born, but not through any fault of your own. It was because he realised he'd been tricked and unfortunately, you were the one he took it out on."

Mr Watson held up his hand. "Can we stop this now? Are

you trying to accuse me of murder because she had a son I knew nothing about?"

"No." Eliza's voice was firm. "If she'd admitted Robert was your son, it would have sullied her reputation and given you a hold over her. No, I've no doubt she would have kept that secret to herself. I do believe, however, that her death is connected to the child you sold and which, as Mrs Scott correctly deduced, was indeed also your son."

"Me?" Mr Carmichael's voice squeaked in the silence. "Is that why she told me to come here? To meet ... this man?"

Eliza was about to respond when Mr Watson stormed to the door. "What utter nonsense, let me out of here." He pushed past the constable, but the young officer caught hold of him and twisted his arm up his back.

"Not so fast, sir."

Sergeant Mitchell marched across the room and escorted Mr Watson to the centre. "If you wouldn't mind staying until this is finished."

"But this is nonsense. In the space of two minutes I've been told I've fathered two sons."

"And you knew nothing about either of them?" Eliza raised an eyebrow.

"Damn right I didn't."

There was a collective gasp around the room.

"Language, Mr Watson." Sergeant Mitchell stepped forward again. "There are ladies present."

"I'm sorry, but this is a huge shock..."

"So it would seem." Eliza breathed a sigh of relief. *I do believe he's telling the truth.* A glance at Miss McGovern confirmed he was.

"So, is he my father?" Mr Carmichael's voice was still an

octave higher than it should have been. "Is that why I'm here?"

Eliza glanced down at the floor. "Mr Carmichael, I can't be certain Mrs Scott had any intention of introducing the two of you; I suspect her real aim was blackmail."

"Blackmail?" Mr Carmichael's face paled, and he looked around for an empty chair.

"I'm afraid so." Eliza paused as she surveyed the room. "I mentioned earlier that Mrs Scott had persuaded Mr Carmichael to meet her in St Giles. To be more precise, she asked him to be on the headland at quarter past two. That begs the question, why did she leave the bench only five minutes before he was due to arrive? The answer is almost certainly because she'd told Mr Carmichael the man and woman he'd always called ma and pa were *not* his real parents. She'd previously written asking him to meet her here, but when he refused, she was determined to do more. To make sure he was where she wanted him on Thursday afternoon, she promised to tell him who his parents were. Whether she would have done is another matter."

Mr Carmichael's head jerked up. "But she promised..."

Eliza placed a hand on his shoulder. "She may have done, but I would say her real aim was to show your father that she really had tracked you down. I doubt she meant any harm to your mother, which is why I'm not convinced she would have told you who they were. No, in my opinion, the whole top and bottom of this was that she wanted to get back at Mr Watson. He'd unknowingly forced her into a loveless marriage with a man who had bullied her child, and all the while he lived happily in the house she thought should be hers."

"That's nonsense," Mr Watson said. "She was as mean to Mr Scott here as his father ever was."

"Maybe over these last few months, but not when he was a child. While he was dependent on her, she was always there for him. It was only once he married, and no longer needed her, that she became vindictive. She'd given up her life for him and he'd thanked her by finding a wife and moving away." Eliza took another sip of her water. "No, this was about revenge. Mrs Scott had a lot of time on her hands living in the middle of nowhere for years, especially once Mr Scott died, and this was when she decided she wanted Clifftop House. Her first letter asking if she could buy it had been rebuffed and so she said she'd tell the village of Mr Watson's *business activities* and his wanton behaviour, in order to force him into selling her the house. But he turned that down, too. As a final attempt, what better way of making him agree than by showing him his son who she'd arranged to be on the headland. He needn't have even left the house to see him, given the views from his kitchen window."

Mr Burns got to his feet. "Whether you're right about this or not, the fact that Mr Watson may have produced two sons and had a successful business doesn't make him a murderer."

"No, you're right, Mr Burns, and this is where we come to your involvement." Mr Burns raised his hands in a shrug before letting them fall onto the bar.

"You see, the thing is, as despicable as Mrs Scott found Mr Watson's behaviour, he was far less troubled by it. In his opinion, he'd done nothing wrong, and no amount of revelations were going to make him sell his home, something he'd already told her in the two letters that he was careful to keep from her solicitor. But the problem with Mrs Scott was that she didn't give up ... and that was her undoing.

"I suspect it was purely coincidental that she saw Mr Burns on the afternoon in question when she was walking to the headland. At the time, she gave no indication of recognising him, but she must have done, and once she knew he was at home, she decided to pay him a visit. She would have known Mr Burns was Mr Watson's oldest friend and perhaps thought he could put some pressure on him before she called at Clifftop House."

Mr Watson's eyes flicked to his friend, but he said nothing.

"Now, I obviously don't know what she said to you that afternoon, Mr Burns, but it must have been enough to make you worried. You didn't want her ousting your friend from his house, only to move herself in. But she was well aware of your past and how dependent you were on Mr Watson, often working with him on his little *endeavours*. What you mustn't have known was that Mr Watson wasn't particularly troubled by her threat. That's why, in the heat of the moment, you tried to shake some sense into her. The problem was, you failed to realise your own strength and squeezing her around the neck really wasn't the most sensible thing to do."

Archie moved to Eliza's side as Mr Burns and Mr Stewart stepped towards her.

"Let's keep this civil, gentlemen."

"Civil? When she's accusing Mr Burns of murder?" Mr Stewart glared at Eliza.

"I'd be quiet if I were you, Mr Stewart, before you talk yourself into being an accomplice."

"Me! I wasn't even there. I was with you ... as you well know."

Eliza pursed her lips. "I do indeed, for the time of the murder at least."

"What's that supposed to mean?"

Eliza studied him. "Let me tell you. We know the cause of death was strangulation, probably at around half past two that afternoon, but the body wasn't discovered until about ten o'clock that night. At that time, it was you who stopped us from checking it was a body we'd seen."

"The tide was coming in!"

"And that provides another clue to all this. At the time of death, it was too early to dispose of the body. I suspect Mr Burns checked the beach, but when there were people on it, he realised he'd have to wait until high tide. While he waited, he moved the body to a corner of the garden where no one would find it and went to Mr Watson's through the back entrance."

Eliza's eyes flicked between Mr Burns and Mr Watson. "Now, a key question in all of this is, was Mr Watson aware of what Mr Burns had done? At first, I was inclined to think he was, particularly as they spent the rest of the afternoon together. There are two very handy gates in your back gardens that allow you to go between each other's houses without being seen. It would be very convenient to retrieve the body from Mr Burns' garden and throw it from the cliff without anyone seeing you."

"But that's not what you think happened?" Mr Watson raised his eyebrows at her.

"No, actually, I don't. It was only earlier today, when I realised what might have happened, that I spoke to the

235

barman here. He remembered last Thursday because it had been an unusual evening, most notably because Mr Watson had left the bar alone."

"You're right, I did." Mr Watson glanced at Mr Burns. "You left early with a fever."

Eliza raised her eyebrows. "A fever that miraculously disappeared once he got home, I would suggest."

"I'm saying nothing." Mr Burns turned back to the bar. "She can't prove anything."

"Maybe not, but there are some here who could provide proof if they were summoned to give evidence under oath."

Mr Stewart shot Eliza a venomous glance. "Don't look at me, I was at home ... hosting a party in your honour."

"I'll admit you couldn't have been with Mr Burns when he threw the body from the cliff, but somehow you knew what he was doing and had even provided the tarpaulin to wrap the body in. Given you weren't at home when we arrived at your house on Thursday evening, I suspect you'd come to the inn early and spoken to Mr Burns. He'd asked for a sheet of tarpaulin and when a suitable amount of money had changed hands, you nipped home and, without Jean seeing you, crept out again to deliver it."

"I knew nothing of the murder." Mr Stewart's eyes were wide. "He didn't tell me why he wanted it."

"Shut up, man." Mr Burns glared at Mr Stewart before downing a shot of Scotch.

Eliza gave a delicate cough. "Perhaps he didn't, but later that evening you saw Mr Burns throw something from the headland. You couldn't be certain what it was, but you must have had your suspicions given the size and shape of the object. I imagine Mr Burns' plan was that the body would land in the water and be carried out to sea. Unfortunately, he hadn't factored in quite how heavy a dead body is and didn't throw it as far as he intended. You, Mr Stewart, realising what had happened, were about to nip out and pull it further down the beach, when Mrs Appleton and I stepped outside and saw it. We could have reached it before the tide covered the beach, but you were adamant we stayed away. It was just unfortunate for you that you were delayed getting back to shore on the Friday morning."

"You don't know what you're talking about."

"In that case, why did you race up the hill to Mr Burns' house once you heard we'd identified the killer? Were you trying to warn him to stay away from here?"

"What? No ... I just wanted to see him."

"When you usually meet him in here at five o'clock, anyway?"

Mr Stewart's eyes pleaded with Sergeant Mitchell. "I did nothing wrong! There's no harm in calling on a neighbour."

"Other than hampering a murder investigation..." Sergeant Mitchell indicated to the constable to handcuff Mr Stewart while he moved towards Mr Burns.

"I think we've heard enough, gentlemen. Mr Burns, I'm arresting you for the murder of Mrs Scott, and Mr Stewart for aiding and abetting the accused in the disposal of the body and for falsifying evidence."

"Don't listen to her, she's made it all up..." Mr Burns glared at Eliza as he struggled with the sergeant.

Eliza shrugged. "I'll admit it started out as guesswork, but as we uncovered the facts, the pieces fell into place. We should have the evidence we need."

Sergeant Mitchell and his constable checked the

handcuffs were secure while Eliza turned around to Archie. She took the glass of sherry he handed to her but froze as her mother-in-law stood up and marched across the room.

"How dare you?" Mrs Thomson slapped Mr Stewart across the face. "You've known all along who murdered Mrs Scott and yet you were happy to let my daughter take the blame."

Jean followed her mother's lead and stormed towards her husband. "How could you?"

"I did it for you..." Mr Stewart's voice squeaked.

"Me?"

"Mr Burns was very generous ... and he would have carried on paying..."

"And you think that was worth sending my sister to the gallows?" Jean turned to Sergeant Mitchell. "Take him away, Sergeant. I never want to see him again."

"Jean..."

Jean hurried back to Maggie, who was in tears at the table, but Mrs Thomson stayed where she was.

"Lock them both up, Sergeant. They don't deserve any mercy. If it wasn't for my daughter-in-law here, you'd have tried my Maggie for murder."

Eliza's jaw dropped as Mrs Thomson threw her arms around her. A second later, she released her grip.

"I didn't think you could do it, but you saved her. She's been so frightened. Thank you."

Eliza closed her mouth as she watched her mother-in-law waddle back to the table where she sat down and embraced her daughters. "It was the least I could do."

"I suppose I should add my thanks." Mr Scott offered

Eliza his hand. "I never had a doubt about Maggie, but ... well, it wasn't always easy to say so ... and we had no proof."

Eliza smiled. "You have Mr Carmichael to thank for providing her alibi. If he hadn't seen her leave the shop, it would have been more difficult to show she was innocent."

Mr Scott extended a hand to Mr Carmichael. "Thank you."

"You're welcome." Mr Carmichael's smile was short-lived before he spoke. "Mrs Thomson, is it true that Mr Scott and I are brothers?"

Mr Watson turned to face them. "I'd like an answer to that, too."

Eliza nodded. "Can't you see the family resemblance? The three of you have the same eyes."

The men studied each other.

"If you say so." Mr Watson patted both sons on the shoulder. "To think my wife and I never had any children and now I have two sons." He shook his head. "It will take some getting used to."

"We've a lot of catching up to do." Mr Scott glanced across at Maggie, who was still in the arms of her ma. "And I need to introduce you to my wife and daughters."

Mr Carmichael smiled. "That would be nice, but first, I've one more question for Mrs Thomson. After all you said, do you know who my ma is?"

Eliza lowered her voice. "I do, but it's not for me to say, especially not in a room full of people."

Mr Carmichael's shoulders sagged. "I understand."

Eliza squeezed his arm. "I'll tell you what, if she wants to see you, I'll bring her to St Andrews in the morning. Will that do?"

Mr Carmichael's smile returned. "It will. For as long as I can remember, I've dreamed of having a ma and pa; I suppose I can manage for one more day." He shook his head. "Who'd have thought that by this time tomorrow I may have a whole family. I can't thank you enough."

CHAPTER TWENTY-FIVE

The sun was high in the sky as the carriage pulled up outside the house on Market Street. Eliza reached for the wrinkled hand next to hers. "Are you sure you're ready for this?"

Miss McGovern nodded. "I am now ... and thank you. I couldn't have faced anyone in the village if you'd told Mr Carmichael about me in front of them."

Eliza smiled. "As I said, it wasn't my place to do that. I'm just thankful that Mr Watson had led such a life that even he couldn't be sure you were the mother."

"You mean I wasn't the only one?" Miss McGovern's eyes widened.

Eliza shrugged. "I can't be certain, but I imagine he was a handsome man back in his youth and probably didn't worry about such things. Even if there were no more children, there may have been other occasions for him to wonder."

"Gracious, I hadn't considered that. When he and Miss Davison got together, people used to say that they were the dream couple, both so attractive and well suited." Miss McGovern's face dropped.

Eliza patted her hand. "That must have been hard for you."

Miss McGovern stared out of the window. "It was one of those things. I'm over it now." She straightened her back. "Shall we go?"

The coachman waited by the open door to help them from the carriage, but Connie settled back in her seat.

"I'll wait here."

Eliza nodded. "I'll only be a minute."

Miss McGovern took a deep breath as Eliza rapped on the door. It was opened a second later by Mr Carmichael looking as if he'd changed into his Sunday best suit. His eyes flicked between the two women.

"Mrs Thomson."

"Mr Carmichael, let me introduce you to Miss McGovern."

Tears welled in his eyes as he looked down at the immaculately dressed old woman. "Ma?"

Miss McGovern nodded, but her words stuck in her throat.

Eliza watched as the two stared at each other. "Can we come in? It will be easier to talk inside. Maybe you could have a cup of tea."

Mr Carmichael was jolted from his trance. "Yes, of course, forgive me. Come this way."

He led them into a small living room at the back of the

house, which, despite the sun, had a fire roaring in the grate. "Please, take a seat while I put the kettle on. I'll be right back."

Eliza waited for him to leave. "I won't stay for tea. You've a lot of catching up to do and I don't want to be in the way."

"That's very thoughtful of you ... but what do I say?"

"I'm sure you'll find the words. Explain how you weren't allowed to keep him, but perhaps tell him about your family. After all, they're his family now, too. Ask after him, as well."

"Yes, you're right. I will."

Eliza was convinced Connie was snoozing when she got back to the carriage.

"Wake up, sleepy."

Connie sat bolt upright. "I am awake, I was just enjoying the sunshine; it's lovely in here."

"Well, it's even nicer outside. Bring your parasol and we can take a walk around St Andrews. We can't be too long, though, I promised Miss McGovern we'd be back within the hour. I thought it was enough for the first visit."

Eliza spoke to the coachman before he helped Connie down from the carriage.

"How did they get on?" Connie asked as they walked towards the seafront.

"They were both so nervous ... and excited. Imagine being Miss McGovern and meeting your son for the first time after fifty years. I'm hoping this will be the first of many visits for her. Unfortunately, Mr Carmichael won't be able to call on her unless she's prepared for tongues to wag."

"I suppose you're right. Do you ever think we'll live in a world where people mind their own business?"

Eliza grimaced. "It's a nice thought, but I hope not. If

everyone kept to themselves, we'd have no one to turn to when we have another murder."

"Well, I hope that doesn't happen again." Connie smiled proudly at her friend. "I don't know how you did it this week ... pulling all those threads together."

"With a lot of good fortune. It's not easy when most of the people are dead. I got my first inkling when we spoke to Miss McGovern and asked her about the birth of Mr Scott. She was horrified when I suggested Mr Watson could be his father, but there was a moment of hesitation ... some realisation that it wasn't beyond the realm of possibility."

Connie stared at Eliza. "How do you notice these things? I was in the same room as you."

Eliza shrugged. "Call it intuition. Anyway, once I realised there was a chance Mr Watson was the father of both boys, everything started falling into place."

"How did you know Mr Burns was the murderer?"

Eliza's eyes sparkled. "It was the wilted evergreens."

"The evergreens?"

Eliza chuckled. "Do you remember when we were in Mr Watson's garden and looked over into Mr Burns', you commented that the plants had died because they hadn't been watered?"

"Yes." Connie's brow furrowed.

"I realised it wasn't due to lack of water. If you looked at them carefully, a number of branches had been broken and the area that had been flattened looked about the right shape and size for Mrs Scott's body to have been hidden there."

"Why didn't you say anything at the time?"

Eliza rolled her eyes. "Because we were in a hurry and you and Archie seemed more interested in the garden than you were in the murder. I needed to get you away. Besides ... it only dawned on me later."

"You!" Connie giggled as she tapped her friend on the arm. "But how did you know Mr Watson wasn't involved?"

"That was a hunch to start with. He'd been so adamant he'd not seen Mrs Scott, I began to believe he was telling the truth. The thing was, if he had nothing to do with it, it would put the blame squarely on Mr Burns. It was only when I spoke to the barman after we'd had tea yesterday afternoon, that he confirmed Mr Burns had left early that night with a fever. He no more had a fever than I did, but it gave Mr Watson an alibi for the evening because the barman remembered him going home alone."

"Yes, of course. But what about Mr Stewart?"

Eliza sighed. "It was his involvement that took the longest to work out. The way he was behaving made me think he knew something, but on the day in question, he was either with us or someone else in the family. It was only as I was looking through my notes again ... as he'd suggested ... that I remembered he hadn't been at home when we'd arrived for the party on the day of the murder. He'd also been very keen to keep us away from the body that evening. If he'd been back from fishing at his usual time on Friday morning, I suspect he'd have removed it before anyone had the chance to find it."

"Really!" Connie gasped. "But how could he even consider defending Mr Burns when he knew Maggie would take the blame?"

"Because of the money. Knowing what Mr Burns had done, he could have blackmailed him for years. That was all he was worried about."

"But poor Jean." Connie's face dropped. "What do you think she'll do now?"

Eliza shook her head. "I don't know. At least she has the boys and they're old enough to take over from Mr Stewart. I imagine once they're over the shock, they'll carry on as before."

"Oh, I do hope so." Connie swirled the parasol on her shoulder as she eyed Eliza. "You're so clever. It's a good job we were here this week or things might have ended very differently."

"They may indeed." Eliza allowed herself a smile. "Not only that, I've even earned some respect from Archie's ma."

Connie laughed. "Your face was a picture last night when she gave you a hug."

Eliza shook her head. "Are you surprised? It's the first time she's been nice to me since we were married. I'm still in shock."

Connie glanced up at the clock on the cathedral in front of them. "It's nearly time we were turning back. We can't spend too long down here if she's hosting a farewell party for us tonight. The guest of honour can't be late."

Eliza groaned. "Don't get excited, I'm sure she'll go off me again when she remembers Archie and Henry are leaving for Moreton on Saturday."

"Well, make the most of it."

Eliza linked her arm through Connie's. "You know what, I think I will."

THANK YOU FOR READING!

I hope you enjoyed the book. If you did, I'd appreciate it if you
could leave a review.

As well as helping the book gain visibility, knowing you
enjoyed it will encourage me to write more books in the series.

To leave a review, go to Amazon and search for VL McBeath
to get to my author page.
Once there, click on *A Scottish Fling* and scroll down to the
review section.

My only plea. Please no spoilers!

Thank You!

AUTHOR'S NOTE AND ACKNOWLEDGEMENTS

Ever since I started reading cozy mysteries, I've recognised that a potential flaw with the genre regards the number of murders that happen in supposedly tranquil village settings.

Agatha Christie solved the problem by giving Miss Marple an extended family and many distant friends to visit. It seemed to work rather well for her and so I've tried to do something similar for Eliza.

If I'm being honest, making Archie Scottish was more down to accident than design, but with his family background established early in the series, a visit to Scotland seemed like an excellent way to get Eliza & Co out of Moreton. Originally, I'd planned on setting the story in St Andrews, a historic town to the northeast of Edinburgh, but when I looked at the geography and size of the town, I realised it wasn't quite what I had in mind.

That was when I came up with St Giles.

It's a fictional village set just along the coast from St Andrews. Near enough to have access to the police, but small enough for most of the villagers to know each other. I decided this would be the ideal setting for a murder, and besides, aren't small villages the sort of places where secrets are best kept hidden?

During the early planning of the book, I didn't envisage having illegitimate children as a theme, but as I worked out the motive for the murder the story developed a life of its own. I found it interesting to remember how differently children born out of wedlock, and their mothers, were treated in the early twentieth century compared with today. Even during my lifetime, I remember the very real shame it brought, not just on the women involved, but their families as well. In an era before formal adoption processes, as in the book, options for women were very limited. I hope that comes across in the story.

As always, I must thank my family and friends for reading various drafts of the book and giving me feedback. I'd also like to thank my wonderful editor, Susan, who checks that the story makes sense and that my punctuation is in the right place! I couldn't have done it without them.

Finally, I'd like to thank you for reading. I hope you enjoyed it. If you did, you might like to look at some of my other books. Further details are on the next page...

ALSO BY VL MCBEATH

Look out for the newsletter that will include details of launch dates and special offers for future books in the series.

To sign up visit: https://www.subscribepage.com/ETI_SignUp

The *Ambition & Destiny* Series

Based on a true story of one family's trials, tribulations and triumphs as they seek their fortune in Victorian-era England.

An *Ambition & Destiny* standalone novel:

The Young Widow

FOLLOW ME

at:

Website:
https://valmcbeath.com

Facebook:
https://www.facebook.com/VLMcBeath

Amazon:
https://www.amazon.com/VL-McBeath/e/B01N2TJWEX/

BookBub:
https://www.bookbub.com/authors/vl-mcbeath

Made in the USA
Coppell, TX
14 November 2021